David Wingate

Annie Weir

And other Poems

David Wingate

Annie Weir
And other Poems

ISBN/EAN: 9783744722391

Printed in Europe, USA, Canada, Australia, Japan

Cover: Foto ©Andreas Hilbeck / pixelio.de

More available books at **www.hansebooks.com**

ANNIE WEIR

AND OTHER POEMS

ANNIE WEIR

AND OTHER POEMS

BY

DAVID WINGATE

WILLIAM BLACKWOOD AND SONS
EDINBURGH AND LONDON
MDCCCLXVI

SCENE.

—

AUTHOR *and* FRIEND *present : between them a table
strewn with MS.*

Friend. These, then, I suppose, are your new Poems.

Author (with a sigh). Yes.

Friend. Where is your Preface ?

Author. I have written none.   I expect you will do that
for me.

Friend. Me, sir !   I don't know what you ought to write
about.

Author. That's precisely my own position.

(*After a pause.*)

It would never do to copy the old one, I suppose !

Friend. Hardly, I am afraid.   They would be sure to
accuse you of poverty in invention, and that would be——

Author. Too near the truth to be pleasant.   But I have
nothing else to say.

Friend. Thank the gentlemen of the Waverley Burns
Club for the interest they have taken in your new Volume.
In particular, thank their Secretary——

Author (*impatiently*). I tell you they don't want thanks, and I question if their Secretary would open the Volume if he suspected it said a word on the subject.

Friend. Well, there are other gentlemen not of the W. B. C. to thank for kind exertions.

Author. Sir, they are all friends who have wrought for love, and they don't want thanks. They know I am grateful.

Friend. What about the Public?

Author. I'm sure I can't tell.

(*A long pause.*)

Friend (*suddenly, with animation*). I have it.

Author. Well?

Friend. Don't write any Preface.

Author (*in great glee*). The very thing. Nobody can object to the style in that case. I don't know how much I am obliged to you.

Friend. Nonsense! I am glad to be of use.

Author. Then we say, No Preface!

Friend. No PREFACE!

CONTENTS.

A N N I E   W E I R

AND ·OTHER POEMS.

ANNIE WEIR.

A TALE.

By a burn, that dimpling crept,
'Neath the leaves that o'er it slept
In the balmy breezeless eve, sat an old man, thin and
    grey,
And two children at his side,
Sunny-faced and merry-eyed,
Aweary with their sport, on the green sward lay:

And while from the poplar tall
Fell the blackbird's madrigal,
While the wagtail on the boulders chirruped near,
And the thrush sang down the dell,
In the thorn above the well,
The story of his youth they sought to hear.

"Uncle Reuben, long ago,
When the fields were white with snow,
And the glen with gleaming icicles was gay,
Well we mind that even then
You went daily from the glen
To sit among the tombs on yonder brae.

"And when the spring had come,
And the bees began to hum,
And morn came with her chalice filled with dew,
Still the graveyard had its charm—
Long you sat, when days were warm,
But why you went at all we never knew.

" Once we asked you why you went,
And what your lingering meant,
Oh ! ' Not to-night,' you answered—' not to-night.'
Would it pain you now to tell,
While yon labour-closing bell
Sounds sweetly, and the sky is golden bright ?

" We'll be silent as the thrush
That is listening in yon bush,
The while her mate with rapture cheers the dale :
Uncle Reuben, will you not ? "
And the old man, so besought,
Assenting, thus began the promised tale :—

" And sae ye wish to ken
Why I daily leave the glen
To spend a lonely hour in the auld kirkyaird,
That nestles 'neath the limes
That, since the olden times,
Hae a solemn shadow flung owre its billowy swaird.

" Be still, and ye shall hear ;
  But if ye hae nae tear
To drop owre sorrow's tale, or sigh to heave,
  Then to your play begone,
  And leave me here alone
To paint anew my heaven—my old dream-web to
  weave.

" Owre bye, near yonder bank,
  Where the coltsfoot's growing rank,
And the binweed thrives where the bere should be ;
  Where the rigs are hower*a* yet,
  Langsyne there was a pit,
And auld anes owre ayont it were twa or three.

" 'Twere owre lang a tale to tell,
  How, in thae times, aft it fell
That sic pits, wi' bounds unmarked, and of water
  brimming fou,
  Were but traps for maids and men ;
  The pent flood now and then,
Wi' ruin in its roar, bursting through.

" In the pit near yonder bank,
Where the coltsfoot grows sae rank,
And the binweed thrives sae weel, 'twas mine to toil ;
And there earth's dearest maid,
Like a glow-worm in the shade,
Made an Eden o' the gloom wi' her smile.

" Oh ! she was fairer far
Than the gowan or the star,
In the green glades o' earth or the blue o' heaven,
And gentler than the dove ;
And her heart's first love,
In its freshness and its faith, to me was given.

" She wasnae seventeen,
But at work she lang had been,
And up the weary stairs wi' her coal-creel laden,[b]
Day by day, wi' trembling limb,
In the twilight dim,[c]
For her frail old father's sake, clamb the peerless
maiden.

" That her silken auburn hair,
    Snawy hauns, and face so fair,
Should be daily soiled sae sair I aye was mourning;
    But my Annie at her wark,
    Aye as lichtsome as the lark,
Gaed singing to the stair, and sang returning.

" Oh ! sweet's the laverock's trill
    In the cloud that crowns the hill,
And the hidden blackbird's sang in the hazel bush at
      e'en;
    But ne'er sae sweet nor dear
    As the sang o' Annie Weir,
In the darkness o' the pit heard—hersel' unseen.

" Ae morn—ae summer morn—
    When white was every thorn—
When the barley braird was silvered wi' the dew,
    Sweet was every scene and soun',
    And but few I mind gaed doun,
But I and Annie Weir were o' the few.

" Frae the ithers far awa'
    We toiled our ainsels twa—
Strange fears that day came owre me now and then ;
    Aften down my pick I flang,
    Listening eerie for her sang,
And thinking she was lang o' coming ben.[d]

    " Tak' yoursels in fancy doun,
    And frae the waste[e] aroun'
Let this sudden cry o' terror strike the ear—
    ' Oh ! the water's broken in !
    To the stair for safety rin !'
And fancy a' the fears o' Annie Weir.

    " She heard the awesome din,
    And she saw the others rin—
She saw them to the stair for safety flee ;
    She heard the distant rush
    O' the water's coming gush,
Looked upward, and the sunshine filled her e'e.
    Her foot was on the stair,
    But, oh ! I wasnae there ;
Sae, flinging aff her creel, she flew for me.

" In the shearing/ I was thrang
Crooning Annie's fav'rite sang
(A lay of humble love and its reward),
When from the silent waste
Cam' the voice o' ane in haste,
And ' Reuben, Reuben, rin !' I wondering heard.

" 'Oh, Reuben, Reuben, rin !
For the water's broken in !—
They a' cam' to the bottom but yoursel'.
Oh ! Reuben, haste ye fast,
For it's coming like a blast,^{g}
And how we're to win oot I canna tell.'

" Though I trusted she was wrang,
Yet I didna tarry lang,
But hurried out my frichted burd to meet,
And we ran to win the stair,
Oh ! but lang ere we were there,
The black and stoury flood^h was at our feet.

" Turning roun' wi' frantic speed
   O' nae danger taking heed,
Through the waste for safety's path we sought in vain,
    Then eerie, bruised and sair,
    Haun' in haun' and in despair,
To the road that best we kent we came again.

" We didna tear our hair,
   But it surely was despair,
That made us ither's hauns sae wildly tak';
    For our heavy hearts aye sunk,
    As wi' hollow, dismal, clunk,
The water slowly rose and drove us back.

" For hope.there was nae room,
   There we saw and kent our doom,
Nae skill, nor faith, nor prayer could scaur't awa,
    It would creep up pace by pace,
    And to reach the farthest face
It could but tak' a day, or maybe twa.

" ' Come, Annie, let's gae ben,
    A' our sorrows soon will en',
For us nae earthly morn can hae a breakin',
        We'll our watch in patience keep—
        Oh ! that we could but sleep,
Ere owre us creeps the flood, and never waken.'

" ' Oh ! Reuben, Reuben Shaw,
    I' the' nae way out ava ?
Wi' this ae feeble light on our white faces streaming,
        Maun we our hopes resign
        And our dear lives tyne ?
Oh ! waefu' waefu' end o' a' our gouden dreaming ! '

" Sae in the first wild hour
    Did we our wailing pour,
Nor thought how e'en the feeble light would fail us ;
        Nor that the flood might stay,
        Far frae us on the brae,
And yet a sterner foe ere lang assail us.

" Let your fancy, if it can,
     Paint us sitting worn and wan,
Watching owre our last bit candle as it flared its dying
        flare ;
     Fled our guardian Angel seemed,
     And till then we had not dreamed,
That ony darker shade could fa' on our despair.

" Like parents owre a child,
     That its hindmost smile hath smiled,
Owre the glowing loveless wick low we leaned wi'
        fondling care,
     And gently blowing strave
     The lowe alive to save,
And chase away the gloom for ae brief moment mair.

" But we gently blew in vain,
     So we raised our een again
At ance, I kenna why nor what we wished to see ;
     But I saw—and see it noo—
     Beaming memory's mazes through,
The old sweet look o' love and trust in Annie's ee.

" But the wick a faint dull red
  In its ain white ase half hid,
Lang glowed and seemed a soul that the Fates were
    loath to sever;
  Then it dwindled to a spark,
  That a star seemed in the dark—
A star that sudden set to rise no more for ever.

" And then no more was seen,
  Save as we strained our een,
To bless our longing hearts wi' anither look o' ither,
  Ae flash we thought we saw,
  But it could be nocht ava',
Save the ee o' frenzied Hope as she left us a'thegither.

" Oh ! ne'er before since Light
  Half his kingdom won frae Night,
Had the darkness of the pit haen a dreariness sae drear;
  For the shadow seemed to clasp
  With a stifling, chilling grasp,
While uncannie feet we heard on the water drawing near.

" How the laneness grew mair lane,

When a' note o' time was gane ;

How our hearts sank now and then, and to die we laid

us doun ;

How the hours crept into days ;

How we prayed and warbled praise,

That wakened in the waste a sadly solemn soun';

" How the hunger pang we bare

When the water was our fare ;

How we tried to be contented with our cheer ;

How the flood rose to our feet ;

How it stood, and durstnae weet

The garments o' the Angel, Annie Weir ;

" How we heard sweet music swell,

If asleep we briefly fell,

And, waking, heard what seemed the hum o' bees ; '

How we closer crept in awe

When the phosphor-light [k] we saw,

That seemed a spirit sitting 'mong the trees ;

" How the old folks were our thought—
How to want they might be brought;
How the God aboon would surely guide them through;
What we would hae done ava,
Had our number no been twa,
And how a solace aye from that we drew;

" How the fearfu' thought that death
Mightnae come at ance to baith,
Made the sore-tried reason reel, and the blood with
horror chill,—
A' this, and mickle mair,
Ye the telling o' maun spare,
For the memory o't awakens horror still.

" But the end at last drew near :
At my side lay Annie Weir,
And murmured lowly, ' Reuben, part maun we.
Oh ! how wearied I hae grown,
Like a hunted bird that's flown,
Despairing, lang, across a biel'less lea.

" ' Oh ! sweet it was to dream
    We at anco should cross the.stream
Whase shores are Earth and Heaven, but 'twinna be ;
    A' my dreaming's been in vain ;
    I the stream maun cross alane,
And ye your weary doom alane maun dree.'

    " Then she seemed asleep to fa',
    And I thought she was awa',
When, hark ! 'twas surely voices in the waste
    (It sae like a fancy seemed,
    That I thought I had but dreamed),—
'Twas the searchers coming cautious in their haste.

    " Frae another, ebber' pit—
    I can tell ye where it's yet—
Three weary days they, hour aboot, had redd; [m]
    Like giants had they toiled,
    And success had on them smiled,
For safely to the sunshine were we led.

" Annie Weir and I were wed,
    But her bloom for aye was fled ;
Ae year she lived, and ere she was a mither,
    She was laid in yon kirkyaird,
    'Neath the greenest o' its swaird,
And oh ! that we were ance again thegither."

A DAY AMANG THE HAWS.

WHEN the beech-nuts fast are drappin',
  And the days are creepin' in,
When ilk carefu' mither's thinkin'
  O' the winter's hose and shoon;
When the mornin' bells loud ringin'
  To the Fast-day worship ca's,
Out comes the city callan'
  For his day amang the haws.
O' the dangers that await him
  Ne'er a troublous thought has he,
Nought cares he for the tearin'
  He his claes is sure to gie;
But the light o' comin' pleasure
  On his heart like sunshine fa's,
For dear as stolen waters
  Is a day amang the haws.

B

Frae the mill where stourie "jennies"
　　Round him aye are whirrin' thrang;
Or the forge where ponderous "Condies"
　　Dunt and dirl the hale day lang;
Or the press-room's inky regions,
　　And the gaffer's cuff and ire;
Or the needle, or the lingle,
　　On he plods through mud and mire.
Frae the lane where Vice holds revel,
　　Where beneath fair Virtue's shield,
Like birds escaped the snarer,
　　Aye a gratefu' few find bield;
Frae the stench that kens nae sweetenin',
　　And the din that has nae pause,
To the freshness and the freedom
　　O' a day amang the haws.

Think ye thus?—"The graceless callan'
　　To the kirk should rather gang;
Does his mither never warn him
　　That sic Fast-day traikin's wrang?

If her heart is for him pleadin',
    Kennin' weel how sair he's wrought,
For the customs o' her faithers
    Has she ne'er a reverend thought?"
Oh, rather thus excuse her :
    " She was born amang the hills,
And she minds the autumn grandeur
    O' the thorns beside the rills ;
There are memories fresh frae girlhood
    Crowdin' fast to plead his cause,
And she canna keep the callan'
    Frae his day amang the haws."

Like a flood the rain's been pourin',
    But the sun beams through at last,
As amang a host o' ithers
    Frae the town he hastens fast ;
On the whinny slopes o' Cathkin,
    Or on Pollock's woody knowes,
He already roams in fancy
    Where he kens the haw-tree grows.

On the bitter blast that's brewin'
  He looks west wi' hopefu' ee,
For he kens the woods frae keepers
  In sic weather will be free.
If the bells around him ringin'
  Whisper whiles o' broken laws,
"Oh!" he thinks, "there's surely pardon
  For ae day amang the haws."

Fu' boldly has he ventured,
  And in darin' weel has thriven,
He the ripest, richest branches
  Frae the sweetest trees has riven.
See his jacket hangs in tatters,
  Owre his hands the bluid-draps steal;
But his mither mends fu' neatly,
  And his scarts again will heal.
Frae his hair the rain is dreepin',
  But he never thinks o' harm,
For Pleasure, wanderin' wi' him,
  Wi' her mantle keeps him warm.

How his heart wi' pride is swellin',
   As he near the city draws,
For he kens he comes joy-laden
   Frae his day amang the haws.

Wha thinks he frae his ramble
   Winna better come, but worse,
Wi' its memory hangin' owre him
   Like an angry father's curse ?
In Nature's face what is there
   That a city bairn should fear ?
In the woodland's autumn whisper
   Is there ought he shouldna hear ?
Wha kens what heavenly music
   May be stirred his breast within,
As the sapless leaf's faint rustlin'
   Turns the sparklin' ee aboon,
While his fancy paints the Painter
   O' the million-tinted shaws,
And the poet-spark is kindled
   In his soul, amang the haws ?

Oh ! keepers, spare the callan'—
   And sweet dreams ye shall not lack—
For the woe things' sake that weary
   Wait the wanderer's coming back ;
They hae shared the city's hardships,
   And o' plenty little ken—
Let them taste in rich abundance
   O' the spoils o' hill and glen.
Owre the priceless feast they'll linger,
   Till their lips and teeth grow brown ;
Or wi' the ruddy treasure
   In their bosoms cuddle down.
Oh, there's nane the joy can measure,
   That a boon sae sma' may cause !
Tears are dried and sorrow's lightened
   Wi' a day amang the haws.

And ye whase lot is coosten
   Aye amang the caller air,
Wha on a gift sae common
   May a thought but seldom wair,

Oh ! think if Heaven had placed ye
   Far frae glen and mountain stream,
Where the woods are things o' fancy,
   And the yorlin's sang a dream—
Oh! think how ye would weary
   But to hear ae laverock sing,
And to watch the matron peesweep
   Chase the hawk wi' daring wing—
How wild would be your longin'
   For the breeze on hills that blaws !
How muckle would ye venture
   For ae day amang the haws !

SONG—LONELY STREAM.

WHEN the ice that hangs adorning
  Yon grey rocks that o'er thee frown,
Loosened in the blaze of morning,
  Gaily glancing, topples down ;
While thy brown flood's foaming free,
Lonely stream, I'll come to thee.

When the wintery tempest, fluting
  'Mong the beeches, o'er thee blows,
Or, the ivied ash uprooting,
  Bridges thee with broken boughs ;
In thy boulder nooks to dream,
Then I'll seek thee, lonely stream.

When the coltsfoot flower is thrusting
  All aside its way that barred ;

When the hawthorn bud is bursting,
   When thy banks are primrose-starred,
While thy linnets chant their glee,
Then be sure I'll come to thee.

A DEATHLESS LOVE.

Oh, sing that plaintive sang, dear May!
  Ance mair ere life I tyne;
There's no in all the world, dear bairn,
  A voice sae sweet as thine.
Alang life's path I've tottered lang,
  The broken arch is near;
And when I fa' I fain would hae
  Thy warbling in my ear.

Oh, sing again that plaintive sang!—
  It waukens memories sweet,
That slumbered in the past afar,
  Whare youth and bairn-time meet.

I roam through woods wi' berries rich,
  Or owre the breezy hills—
Unwearied, wander far to dream
  Beside love-hallowed rills.

Sit owre beside me, winsome bairn,
  And let me kiss thy brow ;
Wi' baith thy warm wee hauns press mine—
  Oh, would the end come now !
Or would—but 'tis a sinfu' wish,
  As sinfu' as it's vain ;
We could not sit for ever thus,
  Nor thou a child remain.

There's nane I love like thee, dear bairn—
  Thou ken'st nae why, I ween :
Thou only hast thy grannie's smile,
  Thou only her blue een ;
Thou only wilt the village maids
  Like her in sang excel ;
Thou only hast her brow and cheek,
  Wi' rosy dimple dell.

It's mony a weary year since she
  Was 'neath the gowans laid,
Yet aft I hear her on the brae,
  And see her waving pláid :
And aften yet, in lanely hours,
  Returns the thrill o' pride
I felt when first we mutual love
  Confessed on Lavern side.

They say there's music in the storm
  That tower and tree o'erturns,
And beauty in the smooring drift
  That hides the glens and burns ;
And mercy in the fate that from
  Our fond embraces tears
The angel o' a happy hame—
  The love o' early years :

But he whase house the storm has wrecked,
  No music hears it breathe.
Wha e'er saw beauty in the drift
  That happed a frien' wi' death ?

Or wha, when Fate wi' ruthless haun',
  His life's ae flower lays low,
Can breathe a grateful prayer, and feel
  There's mercy in the blow ?

Sae thought I when her een I closed ;
  And, though the thought was wrang,
It haunted me when to the fields
  My meals nae mair she brang.
And aften by the lone dyke-side
  A tearfu' grace was sain ;
And aft, alas ! wi' bitter heart,
  The books at e'en I taen.

Nane think how sadly owre my head
  The lang, lang years hae passed—
Nane ken how near its end has crept   .
  The langest and the last ;
But I fu' brawly ken, for, May,
  Your grannie came yestreen,
And joy and hope were in her smile,
  And welcome in her een.

Sit near me, May—sit nearer yet—
    My heart at times stauns still :
'Tis sweet to fa' asleep for aye
    By sic a blithesome rill—
My thoughts are wanderin', bairn.   The veil
    O' heaven aside seems drawn ;
The deepenin' autumn gloamin's turned
    To summer's brightest dawn.

My een grow heavy, May, and dim—
    What unco sounds I hear !
It seems a sweeter voice than thine
    That's croonin' in my ear.
Lean owre me wi' thy grannie's face,
    And waefu' glistenin' ee ;
Lean kindly owre me, bairn, for nane
    Maun close my een but thee.

THE FIRST GUID DAY.

It is the showery April;—
　　The spring-time has begun,
And o' the comin' summer
　　There's a promise in the wun'.
The hawthorn buds are burstin',
　　The birds in chorus gay
A hymn o' thanks are warblin',
　　For the first guid day.
The breeze is warm and westlin',
The firs sae saftly rustlin',
To doves among them nestlin',
　　Say, " Winter's passed away;"
While clouds o' downy lightness
Float on in snowy whiteness,
As if to aid the brightness
　　O' the first guid day.

It is the herald April;—
    The farmer looks abroad,
And thinks how such a sunshine
    Will dry the wettest clod.
Stour-cluds he sees in fancy
    Ahint his harrows play,
While dreams o' wealth are whispered
    By the first guid day.
And see by yonder plantin',
Athort the lea-rigs rantin',
Wi' tails in air tossed, wanton,
    His stirks leap jauntily.
And why are they sae canty
While grass is yet sae scanty?
They feel the coming plenty
    In the first guid day.

It is the buddy April;—
    The roads wi' bairns are thrang,
Whase fairy glee is bursting
    In rude and rapturous sang:

Ilk little face, but lately
    Sae joyless and sae blae,
Is wreathed wi' smiles and roses
    On the first guid day.
And hark ! that gentle hummin',
Frae yonder cottage comin',
Is it the careless thrummin'
    O' fingers skilled to play ?
Oh, no ! it is the singin'
O' bees around it wingin',
The gladsome tidings bringin'
    O' the first guid day.

It is the joyous April ;—
    We feel—we kenna hoo—
As if the world were better,
    · And our lease o' life were new.
Our hearts are beating lightly,
    And on life's brambly brae
The upward path seems smoother,
    On the first guid day.

                    c

The lark on wings untirin',
To reach the lift aspirin',
The bard below is firin',
    To sing a crowning lay.
All nature says, "Be cheery,
O' gladness never weary,
But banish all things eerie
    Frae the first guid day."

GRATITUDE.

O THOU that rul'st the storm, and wisely rein'st
The war-steed Desolation, rescuing
   From his raised hoof the poor,
   Who marked with life our door,
And saved us, God of every good,
Let us before Thee pour our gratitude.

Forgive, O God! the discontent which rose
Within our sinking hearts, when we had seen
   The idle plough fast bound
   In the snow-mantled ground
From weary week to week, and saw
No sign that told us of the coming thaw.

Forgive our lack of faith—the thoughts which oft,
In murmuring speech expressed, told all who heard
   That we had ceased to see
   Omniscience in Thee,
And dared to turn our eyes above
And doubt Thy goodness and preserving love.

We saw a happier race speed daily forth
To pleasure on the lakes, returning thence
   With feasting, cups, and song,
   The evening to prolong ;—
That made our little nothing less,
But all our thoughts were thoughts of bitterness.

The robin sat upon our sill and sang,
Like one that hoped, though hungry; but in us
   His heaven-taught melody
   No hope inspired, for we,
The while we listened to his strain,
Thought of our wants, and of the snow-hid drain.

But suddenly Thou bad'st the warm winds blow,
And down the flood came sweeping.   Tiny streams
  The storm-chained plough unbound,
  And coltsfoot flowers were found,
And larks the showery mornings hailed,
And all the hills appeared again unveiled;

And the green fields were softened, and our spades
Were labour-polished; glowed with toil our hands,
  And plenteous, though poor,
  The morning meal came sure;
Our children answered to our call,
A little thinner each, but living all.

THE STREAMLET.

LATELY in the songless gloaming
  Of a sunny winter day,
Strolled I by a stream that, nameless—
Free from finny tribes, and fameless—
  Wandered on its Clydeward way.

Vacantly its windings tracing,
  From its freshness nought I sought—
Nothing wished in verse to treasure;
Love, or hate, or care, or pleasure,
  Won or craved no passing thought.

Like a lullaby its music
  Rose beside me, and my soul,
To resist its spell unarmoured,
Scarcely hearing that it murmured,
  Yielded to its soft control.

Like a dreamless midnight slumber,
　Fruitless, passed the flying hour;
Memory kept her lamp extinguished,
Fancy, for the hour, relinquished
　All its world-creating power.

Nought I of the young moon's presence
　Nor the first star's rising knew,
Till a robin, like a spirit—
I could less observe than hear it—
　Close before me flitting flew.

Suddenly the darkness deepened,
　Presence to the moon was given,
Night's first star was twinkling o'er me,
Burning mine-heaps glared before me
　On the knowes, like Mars in heaven.

Trees that slept as erst I passed them,
　Now to graceful wavings stirred,
For my reverie was broken—
Some all-potent charm was spoken
　In the flitting of that bird.

And the stream itself, how altered!
Full of life it onward dashed,
Music mingled with its wimple,
Moons and stars in every dimple
　Broke and shimmered, danced and flashed.

"In its babble there's a sermon,"
　Muttered I, and straight began,
Nothing of my folly weening,
Something of its hidden meaning
　To interpret, as it ran.

Pausing oft, intently listening,
　All my wits to work were thrown;
But the language of its streaming,
Though of most familiar seeming,
　Was to me a thing unknown.

Yet the low and dreamy murmur
　Of its dimly rippling flow,
And the whisper of its laving,
Round the last year's rushes waving
　In the shadow, to and fro,

Would not from my thoughts be driven—
    Would like human sayings seem,
Though the language of its streaming
Did not seem so much the dreaming
    As the reading of a dream.

" Yes," I said, " there is a sermon
    Uttered in its gentle roll;
But I must interpret poorly,
For the strange-tongued talker surely
    Speaks the promptings of my soul."

Then away my memory wandered
    Slowly, far along the past;
Boyhood ventures and achievements,
Manhood's troubles and bereavements,
    Came before me crowding fast.

And the while my memory travelled
    Early love and joys among,
Lo ! the stream a lyric quoted—
Syllables and rhymes I noted—
    And I knew the song it sung.

Never was there such a preacher!
   Now my soul was filled with glee;
Smitten now with fear and wonder,
When aloud it seemed to thunder
   Things but known to Heaven and me.

Now 'tis an accusing spirit,
   Torturing while it holds in thrall—
· Like an angry eye it glistens,
No delightful reminiscence
   Suffering memory to recall;

' Now a flattering nymph, my merits
   Telling o'er with Siren art—
Could a meed so sweetly numbered
Leave asleep the pride that slumbered
   Cloaked and hidden in my heart?

Now while round its boulders rushing,
   Witch-like, in my ears it dinned
Thoughts of suicide once uttered,
Curses deep in madness muttered,
   Tales of sins in secret sinned;

Feelings nourished in the struggle
  For existence, o'er it conned;
" Mine's a care that has no waning,
Sin is not in *my* complaining,"
  Like a weary slave it groaned.

Then, while with an almost voiceless
  Motion gliding underneath,
Budless brambles o'er it bending,
From its breast there seemed ascending
  Wailings of decay and death.

Lispings of long-silent voices
  Thrilled me; and four names most dear
(Whispered low in anguished falter),
Agnes, Mary, Catherine, Walter,
  In its murmur I could hear.

Then where rounded pebbles glistened,
  Scarcely covered in the stream,
All its sweetly murmured story
Was of love, and hope, and glory,
  Brighter than the brightest dream.

.   .   .   .   .   .

Musing as I homeward hasted
   Through Garscadden's flowerless vales,
This appeared a truth the surest—
They whose hearts and lives are purest,
   Hear from streams the sweetest tales.

GIBBIE'S LAMENT.

DEAR Bessie, owre my dreary cell
    Again has gloomed the night ;
The sulky jailer has been roun'
    And ta'en away my light.
Baith heaven and earth seem fled, and through
    The winnock at my side
I vainly gaze—the verra stars
    Frae me their faces hide.

The hale day lang I've pingled owre
    That heap o' tautit tow,
And thought my burning finger-nebs
    Wad sotten't in a low.
And oh I'm sure I wish they had—
    The thought may weel be wrang,
But patience comes but seldom here,
    And never tarries lang.

Oh, Bessie, could you through thae wa's
　　Your faithfu' Gibbie see,
I'm sure your heart wad burst in sabs,
　　Your tears would blear your e'e ;
To think that I sae cauld should lie,
　　My bed as hard's a stane,
Wi' no a living thing except
　　The cloks to hear my mane.

Were I a swindler or a thief
　　This cell would be my pride,
There canna be a better place
　　Frae a' the world to hide ;
But I've nae skill to steal or cheat,
　　Yet here I'm forced to stay :
I've thought on't, Bessie, till I fear
　　My thoughts are gaun agley.

My head is turnin', Bessie dear ;
　　I ken I'm wauken wide,
And yet I see ye wi' the bairns
　　Here stannin' at my side.

Your breath is on my cheek, your haun'
    Upon my face I fin'—
It's passin' owre my shirpet chafts,
    And een sae far faun in.

But yesterday I waled me out
    A tuft o' tow sae fine,
And sat me doun, wi' mournfu' pride,
    To plait a fishin'-line ;
And had I haen but ae wee swirl
    O' thy saft gouden hair,
I would hae bow't a preen, and tied
    A yellow flee fu' rare.

And, Bessie, on my bed I sat
    And thought the floor a stream,
And siller grilse and gouden trout
    Were soomin' through my dream,
When in the prowlin' jailer cam'—
    The fiend was in his e'e ;
And, Bessie, with the supper-hour
    Nae supper cam' to me.

Oh, Bessie, to the water side
  At dewy gloamin' steal,
And in your faithfu' Gibbie's name
  Bid a' the streams fareweel.
For me, I'll never see them mair;
  I hear a voice that says—
" Life's pirn's unwinding fast; ye'll ne'er
  Wun through thae sixty days."

VERSES

TO A (SUPPOSED) FOSSIL FISH.

[The following verses were suggested by a ball of ironstone, of a
very fish-like shape, which was brought into the School of Mines,
Glasgow, and which it was thought would prove one of the family
of coal saurians, two of which have been found in the coal-measures
of the carboniferous system.   It proved to be no fish, however.]

AND didst thou once frequent the sea
A living creature—could it be ?
Let me wi' reverence lean owre thee
    And view ilk part ;
A wonder in the first degree
    Thou surely art.

Oh, what a graceless form is thine !
Was that contorted ridge thy spine ?
Did bony plates thy flesh confine,
    Or wrinkled scale ?
Did at that fracture smooth once join
    A lang lithe tail ?

D

Thy venturous path how didst thou guide
Throughout the wonder-peopled tide ?
No trace of fin at back or side
       Dost thou display :
Did gills the needfu' air provide,
         Or nostrils, pray ?

Strange creature of the auld-world brine,
Was this thy living form's outline ?
Did at that oval mark once shine
       A lashless e'e ?
And didst thou other parts combine
         Than those we see ?

Thou syllable in truth's narration,
Were sedgy shores thy habitation ?
In life's unmeasured roll thy station
       We fain would know.
Say, in the morning of creation
         What part played thou ?

Wert thou a thing of blood, to whom
The weaker tribes gave ample room ?
That stony wame their living tomb—
        Preserve us a' !
What thousands may have met their doom
        Within that maw !

Perhaps thou never saw the sea,
And lived from blood and murder free;
Thy home some tideless pool might be,
        Deep fringed with heath,
Which, drying, 'mang its weeds left thee
        In deathless death.

How came it that thou wert encased
Langsyne within the weedy paste,
Where calamites and tree-ferns chaste
        Luxuriant waved ?
What pickle strange from utter waste
        Thy being saved ?

When sound could penetrate thy ear
What awful voices thou wouldst hear,
As o'er the estuary drear
              The storm would roar,
While huge amphibians sought in fear
              The hutless shore.

When life was thine, no human wile
Could to destruction thee beguile ;
The fisher's art and hunter's toil
              Were yet to be ;
And maybe aft since then our isle
              'S been 'neath the sea.

I need not ask thee if thou e'er
The wild bird's morning song didst hear,
Around thee swelling far and near;
              For though their glee
The loneliest human heart would cheer,
              'Twas nought to thee.

Besides, 'tis maybe true that then
No wild birds warbled in the glen,
And morn unhailed rose o'er the fen
        From year to year ;
For music shunned the world till men
        Her voice could hear.

And yet, half-shocked, the fancy says,
'Tis strange if even those far days—
While rarest flowers adorned the braes
        And ferns the plain—
The earth should have no birds to raise
        The praiseful strain.

Say, do they madly theorise
Who say our form from thine doth rise ?
Art thou our father in disguise ?
        It may be true,
There yet a faint resemblance lies
        About the mou'.

Thou etching of a wondrous plan,
What are our wizzen'd mummies gran'
Compared to thee, whose life-stream ran,
                    Syne ceased to flow,
Long cycles ere there was a man
                    To mak' ane o'.

But I may guess till doomsday bell
Shall ring the world's departing knell,
And aye return frae truth's deep well
                    With empty pail,
Unless thou deign'st to rise thysel'
                    And tell thy tale.

THE MARIGOLD.

I KEN a sweet spot where the marigold blooms,
  And pinkies breathe balm in their season,
Where the rambler may roam frae the dawn to the
    gloam,
  And no churlish laird ask the reason.
There the lark a' day lang trills his lady-love's praise,
  And wagtails their mates seek to gladden,
While the burn wimples doun wi' a saft singin' soun'
  Through the gowany howes o' Garscadden.

Weel kent is the spot where the marigold blooms,
  The peesweep's wild pæan sounds o'er it;
The goldie secure 'mang the whins has her nest,
  The wren 'neath the bracken before it.

Dear, dear is it aye to the bright bonny burn,
    Sae blithely its seaward way haudin',
And dear to the shilfa aboon it that broods
    In the balmy haw-bloom o' Garscadden.

Oh, bleak was the spot where the marigold blooms
    When the March winds were blustering around it ;
And bleak when the burn ceased to wimple and sing
    In the grasp o' the ice-king that bound it.
'Twas nae place to gang wi' a fou heavy heart,
    For care there the mair seemed to madden ;
But spring wi' a bound comes to brighten and soothe
    The homes and the hearts o' Garscadden.

To the sweet modest pinkie lang faithfu' I've been,
    O' singin' its praise never weary,
And seeking at gloaming its home on the fen,
    As ane seeks the home o' his dearie.
And now in my eild I've grown fickle, I ween,
    Transferring my warmest applaudin';
But nowhere on earth is sic marigold bloom
    As among the green howes o' Garscadden.

JOHN FROST.

SUGGESTED BY THE PRATTLE OF A CHILD.

Oh, mither, John Frost cam' yestreen,
And owre a' the garden he's been ;
    He's on the kail-stocks,
    And my twa printit frocks
That Mary left out on the green,
        Yestreen,
John Frost foun' them out on the green.

And he's been on the trees, the auld loon,
And heaps o' brown leaves shooken doun;
    He's been fleein' a' nicht,
    Frae the dark to the licht,
And missed nae a house in the toun,
        The auld loun—
He's missed nae a house in the toun.

And, mither, he's killed every flee—
Noo ane on the wa's ye'll no see ;
  On the windows there's nane,
  For the last leevin' ane
Fell doun frae the rape in oor tea,
   Puir thing !—
Just drappit doun dead in oor tea.

And, mither, the path's frostit a' ;
If ye gang the least fast ye jist fa'.
  Oh, ye ne'er saw sic fun !
  I got ae curran'-bun,
And wee Annie Kenzie got twa,
   Daft wee thing ;
She jist slade a wee bit and got twa.

And my auntie her een couldnae close,
For she said her auld bluid he just froze.
  He cam' in below the claes,
  And he nippit oor taes—
And he maist taen awa' Bobby's nose,
   Puir wee man ;
Sure, he couldnae dae wantin' his nose.

And my uncle was chitterin' to death,
And John Frost wadna let him get breath ;
  And the fire wadna heat
  Uncle's twa starvin' feet,
Till the soles o' his socks were burned baith,
   Birslet brown,
And the reek comin' oot o' them baith.

But what brings John Frost here ava,
Wi' his frost and his cranreugh and snaw ?
  It's a bonny-like thing !
  He just waff't his lang wing,
And a' oor wee flowers flew awa',
   Every ane ;
And Ross's red dawlies and a'.

And, mither, he gangs through the street,
Just looking for weans wi' bare feet ;
  And he nips at their heels,
  And the skin aff them peels,
And thinks it's fine fun when they greet,
   The auld loon ;
He nips them the mair when they greet.

Wi' his capers the folk shouldna thole.

D'ye ken?—He breathed in through a bole

Whare a wee lassie lay,

And she dee't the next day,

And they laid her doun in the kirk-hole,

Puir wee lamb—

And covered her in the kirk-hole.

But guess what my auntie tell't me?

She says the wee weans, when they dee,

Flee awa' owre the moon,

And need nae claes nor shoon,

To a place whare John Frost they'll ne'er see,

Far awa'—

To a place whare John Frost daurna be.

And she says our wee Katie gaed there,

And she'll never be hoastin' nae mair.

Sure, we'll gang there ana'—

We'll flee up an' no fa'—

And we'll see her jist in her wee chair—

And she'll lauch

In her bonny wee red-cushioned chair.

AULD ARCHIE BELL.

AULD Archie Bell has his hame in Rockneuk,
He's honest, and douce, and a wabster o' pluck ;
And, born a' the rest o' the world to excel,
Unmatched wi' his shuttle was auld Archie Bell.

But Archie, wha has in the parish a name,
To weavin' alone wasnae bound for his fame ;
No ae thing, nor twa things, could Archie do weel,
For a' bodies owned him a gey clever chiel.
And mony a braw lassie, though ne'er ownin' why,
For Archie would sigh, and her supper lay by—
Na, ladies, 'twas said, frae the Duke's and Dalziel,
Glanced love frae their carriage on auld Archie Bell.

There wasnae a loon in the hale country roun',
But in a lang race Archie Bell could rin doun ;

And if he at sports ne'er a prize could display,
'Twas only because he was pleased to hae't sae—
On's fours he could rin wi' the speed o' a grew,*
Owre hurdles, yard high, like a lintie he flew :
And whether restricted to gallop or trot,
'Twas a' ane to Archie, he cared nae a grot.

When Reynard was roused frae the glen o' Dalziel,
Wi' the barkin' o' hounds and a wild human yell,
Where'er the chase led them, be't foul day or fair,
Wi' his shoon in his oxter auld Archie was there—
The chief dread o' Reynard, the soul o' the hunt,
Owre hedges and ditches he spankit in front :
The horses might fag—dogs lie doun oot o' breath—
But Archie ne'er failed to be in at the death.

In Archie's lithe bouk there was nae needless length,
And the bend at his knees was a token o' strength ;
He could spin like a peerie through lang Highland reels,
And dump like a black on the floor wi' his heels.

                    * Greyhound.

Wi' Archie's wild "hooch!" and his still wilder screigh,
E'en bridegrooms at weddings ne'er thought the hours
    dreigh;
And the fiercest o' waps wi' ae cry he could quell,
For the lungs o' a lion had auld Archie Bell.

But wha a' the feats o' his youth could rehearse ?—
E'en the meed o' his eild soars aboon my poor verse :
How he wooed, how he won, though the battle was hard,
The bonniest lass in the whole Middle Ward;
How in hard times he turned owre the green orchard sod;
How he wrocht wi' the masons and carried the hod ;
How the mortar he mixed, spite o' frosts and wet thaws,
Will bind and haud fast till the last trumpet blaws.

Nae mortal wi' Archie can fettle bee-skeps,
And wide is the fame o' his windlestrae caps ;
The bees as he shears them wi' music him cheer,
And the bee-farmers after them come far and near.
There ne'er was a tinkler that e'er wandered by,
Wi' him heather-besoms or house-brooms could tie ;

And Dalziel's famous curlers to own think nae shame
That Archie's braw cowes are the half o' their game.

Ae fondness has Archie :—In sunshine and mirk
He longs to be bedral o's ain parish-kirk.
To him that's sae honoured he wishes nae ill,
But just he would like sic a station to fill.
To ken every bane in the mools o' Dalziel,
And every Lord's mornin' to ring the kirk-bell,
And bear the Guid Books up the auld pu'pit stair—
Ye powers ! grant him that, and he'll fash ye nae mair !

He every heigh grave would smooth down by degrees,
And plant a' the borders wi' flowers and wee trees ;
And wi' an e'e hameward—there's nae sin in that—
Hae cabbage and kail here and there for the pat.
A pattern to a' future bedrals 'twould be :
Auld folk to be laid in't would weary to dee ;
And the saunts that frae't rise at the great day o' grace,
Would swither ere wanderin' frae sic a braw place.

Lang life to ye, Archie ! may sorrow nor care
Ne'er alter the tint o' your ever snod hair :
Secure may ye sit, 'mid the world's din and strife,
Wi' a pension to brighten the gloamin' o' life.
If, ere ye're a bedral, ye're laid in your grave,
For guidsake lie still till ye're roused wi' the lave ;
And dinna, wi' openin' auld graves in the nicht,
Or ringin' the bell, kill the parish wi' fricht.

A CANDLEMAS RHYME.

It was the eve of Candlemas, and in her easy-chair
Sweet Mrs Cameron knitting sat with thrifty zeal and
care ;
And silent sat, in slippered ease, her lord, of portly
frame,
And sturdy Cameronian faith, and stainless local fame.

And on that eve of Candlemas, if memory reckoned
fair,
'Twas sixteen years since they were wed, a humble
hopeful pair,
Rich only in a love that ne'er by coldness had been
crossed,
And theirs was now the beinest house that Lavernshaw could boast.

Full blithe was Mrs Cameron—and wherefore should
    not she?
For where were six such blithesome bairns to keep a
    house in glee?
'Twas true there should another been, but Heaven had
    deemed it best
To make their first an angel, and the guardian of the
    rest.

And as the children played, she let her happy fancy
    roam,
And saw in summer loveliness her childhood's moor-
    land home;
And memory brought its store of joys, and garrulous
    she grew,
And talked of pleasant times that were ere Lavern-
    shaw she knew.

" Ah ! bairns," she said, " this was an eve that, thirty
    years ago,
To every one at school aye passed full wearily and slow,

Because to-morrow was a day when all went blithe to
    school—
A day on which the master stooped to laugh and play
    the fool.

"Oh! dear, dear gala-time! There were no dreary tasks
    that day,
No grim ferule upon the desk in leathern terror lay,
But trays with sweeties richly heaped to fill its place
    were seen,
With pyramids of oranges in order ranged between.

" And, oh ! how graciously our gifts the happy master
    took,
And smiled as if its wonted frown his face no more
    could brook.
Nor less the widow's child received, who laid her
    penny down,
Than she, the daughter of the Laird, who gave her
    silver crown.

" And, oh ! what glorious liberty that day conferred on
    all !

Ours seemed the mirth of slaves relieved from long and
    hopeless thrall ;

The watch-dog barked, and spiders from their nooks
    crept out to hear

That laughter which shook down the dust no more
    than once a-year.

" And well I mind how every year the master spoke a
    speech,

The same one still—his voice seems yet my startled
    ear to reach ;

How I with terror quaking sat, as with a madlike pace

He stamped about the floor, and still waxed redder in
    the face.

" I knew not then what speech he spoke, nor why, he
    spoke so loud,

And waxed so fiery in the face, and seemed so fierce
    and proud,

But wondered aye why such a storm should follow
such a calm,

And the ferule in fancy felt once more upon my palm.

" And sweet was the relief when he had through his
passion toiled,

And panting stood, and wiped his brow, and on his
audience smiled.

And, doubtless, when we cheered he thought our judgment sage and good,

And was convinced his " Norval " for our minds was
proper food.

" And then he told us who was king, and told us who
was queen—

And queen and king were always those whose gifts had
greatest been ;

I ne'er was queen, nor hoped to be, for father's folks
were poor,

And silver crowns were scant among the cottars on the
moor.

" Then on the shoulders of the boys their happy king
    was seen,
And homeward singing as we went, we bore our blush-
    ing queen ;
And Jealousy among us walked, and Envy told her tale,
And so, although we knew it not, we bowed the knee
    to Baal."

So garruled Mrs Cameron, but still her portly lord,
As if the past had charmed him, sat, nor cheered her
    with a word.
To-morrow and its vast affairs had on him laid their
    yoke,
And hard he smoked, and much he thought, and thus
    at length he spoke.

SECOND.

" Rebecca, seek my gouden studs and newest velvet
    vest,
To-morrow's nomination-day, and I must wear my best ;

To-morrow's nomination-day, the battle will be keen,
But ye shall be the Provost's wife before to-morrow's
  e'en.

"And ye shall be the Provost's wife—Rebecca, hear ye
  that ?
And ye shall hae a Paisley plaid, the best that e'er ye
  gat,
And ye'll a velvet bonnet wear, with feathers waving
  braw,
And ye shall wear the grandest gown in bonny Lavernshaw."

" John Cameron, John Cameron, my heart to hear ye's
  sair,
On worldly honours vain and vile a thought why
  should ye wair ?
Let him wha likes be provost, John, since they sic
  things maun hae,
A Cameronian can but smile at all their vain display."

" And wherefore should I change, gudewife? come
    honours as they will,
In faith, as in affection, I will be John Cameron still ;
But I'll be in the provost's chair before to-morrow's
    e'en,
And we in bonny Lavernshaw shall reign a king and
    queen."

" John Cameron, John Cameron, the Tempter's with ye
    been,
And ye hae yielded to his wiles with little strife, I ween ;
Gang to your closet, John—oh ! gang, and grace seek
    frae aboon,
Ye maunna let the morning sun salute you in your sin.

" Why mind ye their elections, John—would ye dis-
    pense their law?
The Council or the Provost's chair is no for you ava ;
The oath of loyalty and love ye could not dare to swear,
And at the table of the Lord's communion syne appear."

" Rebecca, hear ye me.   The town has business to be
   done,
And maun hae men to rule, or things would a' to ruin
   rin ;
My duty in the kirk I've done, and so I hope will do,
But surely one may serve the Lord, and serve his
   country too."

" Look out, John Cameron !   Behold !   God's smile
   is on the earth,
The laverock and the blackbird join to hail the snow-
   drop's birth.
We've seen another spring—let us be thankful for the
   boon,
Nor dare with black apostasy to woo His vengeance
   doon."

"With black apostasy, gudewife, what can ye mean
   ava ?
Our faith is in the synod's care—'tis theirs to give us
   law ;

The testimony of our sires they to the winds have
  thrown,
And that they well and wisely did, have well and
  wisely shown.

" Now to the Queen my loyalty and love I'm free to
  swear,
And I amang the Volunteers a captain's coat may
  wear.
That testimony was a dyke that cowards hid behind,
No coward I'm, and blithe am I 'twas thrown unto the
  wind."

" But, John, among the Synod, though it seems o'
  grace bereft,
E'en there, like Lot in Sodom, is a faithfu' remnant
  left;
Let them·be our example, let us link our lot with
  theirs,
And ye shall be a captain in a band that fight wi'
  prayers.

" Or if the worldly weapon's raised, as in the days of
　　yore,

John Cameron, there's the good broadsword your faith-
　　ful fathers wore ;

Would they to thrones of sin an oath more sinfu' still
　　have sworn ?

For them wha scorn the Covenant would they a sword
　　have borne ? "

" The Covenant and household swords were weel in
　　times awa',

When martyrs won their crowns, and kings had no re-
　　spect for law ;

But every heart is loyal now, and some maun provosts
　　be,

Or Britain wouldnae lang be found the country o' the
　　free."

" John Cameron, John Cameron, our angel bairn I
　　see,

And there is sorrow on her face that was not wont
　　to be ;

Oh, wherefore, owre a bairn in heaven, should hang
    that cloud o' care?
Can one so innocent as she be ought but happy
    there ?

" Oh ! maybe on the book of life a moment she has
    gazed,
And maybe she has seen the name o' ane she loves
    erased.
Some sin o' mine, or thine, gudeman, her peace has frac
    her riven,
And oh ! how foul maun be the sin that taints the joys
    o' heaven."

" It may be sae, wha kens ?—but I my gouden studs
    maun wear ;
And I maun think about a speech to please the public
    ear.
Our angel bairn will smile belyve—Rebecca, so shall
    ye,
And be as proud and happy as a Provost's wife should
    be."

.

SEQUEL.

IT is the eve of Candlemas, the laverock has been
    up,
And from the garden-borders peeps the golden crocus
    cup;
Bright clouds, that seem of summer, from the west
    creep o'er the moon,
And the weather-prophets mutter, "We have spring a
    month too soon."

It is the eve of Candlemas, and in her easy-chair,
Sweet Mrs Cameron knitting sits, unscathed by time
    or care;
The hours have passed on fairy feet, the chapter has
    been read,
And all the Word suggested has in homely phrase been
    said.

Unchanged the household seems, save that a sweeter
    rose has blown
Upon their eldest's cheek, and save that John has
    greyer grown.
'Tis true he straighter sits, and has a more important air,
And there's a military frizz about his beard and hair.

And well may he important seem—he's Provost Came-
    ron now,
And "sitteth in the judgment-seat," with wisdom-
    laden brow;
And yon's a captain's sword that hangs beside the rusty
    blade,
That for the Covenant was drawn at Rullion's bloody
    raid.

And is there then no hidden change, no hardening of
    the heart?
No grudging of the minutes to devotion set apart?
Sprung up around their honours is there not a waste of
    cares,
In which the angels read again the story of the tares?

Oh, no !—the yoke of riches has by them been lightly
 borne,

The roses of their honours have no peace-destroying
 thorn :

They from the war of creeds to live apart have nobly
 striven,

And in a grander company they climb the hill of
 heaven.

A MOTHER'S WAIL.

Oh, Jamie, Jamie, let me greet,
　　Your kindness cheers nae mair ;
I canna dry my tears at will,
　　Nor frae me fling my care.
I ken your ain heart's sad, for she
　　Was sunshine in your e'e ;
But yours is but a father's love,
　　And ye maun bear wi' me.

Oh, Jamie, let me greet—my heart
　　Is sad as sorrow's sel' ;
It seems but yesterday our tears
　　On Willie's cauld face fell.

F

We thocht our lot was hard when Death
  Ae bairn had taen awa' ;
But, oh ! it's muckle harder noo,
  When we hae nane ava.

Had Heaven been pleased to warn us
  O' the blow that was to fa',
And, lichtly leanin', let her dwine,
  As Willie dwined awa',
We micht hae schooled our hearts to bide
  The fate we couldna flee,
And waited, wi' a patient grief,
  To close our darling's e'e :

But, oh ! without a gloamin',
  Fell bereavement's gloom at last—
Wi' scarce a rustle o' its wings
  Awa' her spirit passed.
Though hopefu' seemed her cheek's new bloom,
  And hale her e'e's blithe licht,
'Twas but the clearness o' the sky
  When fa's the April blicht.

She wasna like anither bairn,
   Whase prattlin's nocht but din ;
For there was wisdom in her words,
   Far, far her years aboon.
And whiles sic startlin' things she speired,
   That in my heart I've sain,—
An angel, watchin' owre our souls,
   Is speakin' in my wean.

And ance wi' sparklin' een she sat,
   And at the lift gazed lang,
And speired, when I nae sang could hear,
   " Wha sings that bonny sang ?"
And yet, alas ! we saw nae sign ;
   For hard were we to learn
That a' our love would fail to shield
   Frae death our only bairn.

She aye was at my foot, Jamie,
   And whiles I fashed awee,
When, maybe at my thrangest time,
   She grat to get my knee.

And butt and ben, and oot and in,
    To toddle was her pride—
The dear wee lamb ! she couldna bear
    To leave her mither's side.

Oh, Jamie, twa lang days I've watched
    Her wee white face in vain ;
My longing brings nae warmth—her smile
    Will ne'er return again.
'Twas some sad solace on her brow
    At times to lay my hauns ;
But bleak will be the morning,
    On a bairnless hearth that dawns.

She'll lie in Willie's grave, Jamie :
    Oh ! come nae soon awa',
But wait and smooth the turf, and drap
    A tear aboon the twa ;
For if, as weel they may, they should
    Unseen be lingering near,
'Twill cheer them even in heaven to mind
    Their father's parting tear.

TO A LARK,

ON HEARING ONE SING EARLY IN FEBRUARY.

Up in the sky, sweet lark! Up! up!
  The sun Kilpatrick braes doth brighten,
The care-draught brimming in my cup
  Thou sweetenest, and my heart doth lighten.
Up, and thy first spring-lay prolong;
The labour-ache flies from thy song.

A little higher, lark! No eye
  On earth should see thine eye's joy-glisten;
Hide in yon blue spot of the sky,
  And I'll beneath thee watch and listen;
For if thy voice but reach my ear,
Sweet bird, no other sound I'll hear.

From yonder busy mine but now
  Emerging, I was murmurs muttering;
In vain the sunshine touched my brow,
  Till from the grass I saw thee fluttering,
And heard thy "Hail, Spring!" o'er me burst,
Sweet as the water-spring to thirst.

I foolishly and faithless deemed
  These knowes had nought my heart to gladden;
And nursing discontent, but dreamed
  Of toil and trouble in Garscadden;
Till, like the sun a cloud dispelling,
Thy song came better things foretelling.

What was it called thee up to sing?
  The merle and thrush thy song hear mutely;
Yon frozen uplands feel no Spring;
  The winds with chilling breath salute me.
Say, wherefore didst thou soar so proudly,
And trill thy ecstasy so loudly?

Didst thou perceive the care-cloud spread
  Upon my face, and, sympathising,
Spring from the grey turf, kindness-led,
  And on thy angel-mission rising,
Above me hovered trilling, trilling,
My soul with peace and gladness filling?

Or wert thou only love-inspired,
  Of thy own pleasure thinking only?
Nor looked where I so vexed and tired,
  Among the pit-wood sat so lonely?
And had the song, so sung and heard,
A sensual source alone, dear bird?

'Tis said thou hast no joys of thought—
  That raptureless from earth thou springest;
And thus melodious toiling, nought
  For sunshine car'st, and aimless singest;
And art at most a feathered creature—
A whistle in the mouth of nature.

But thou, sweet bird, art of the seers,
　To whom a wondrous foresight's given,
And when to men no sign appears,
　Thou, in the calendar of Heaven,
Spring's advent read'st, and with weird skill
Her footprint not'st on holm and hill.

And whatsoever else thou art—
　Where'er celestial sages rank thee—
The tribute of one grateful heart
　Thou hast; with all my soul I thank thee.
Where spring ne'er comes, where none can hear
　　thee,
The memory of thy song shall cheer me.

THE CROWS' CHORUS.

Caw ! caw ! the frost's awa' ;
The river is full of the melted snaw ;
The burn foams in flood through the blithseome shaw,
And pickings are plenty—caw-caw, caw-caw !

Nae mair we're weak-winged wi' our scanty fare ;
The clown wi' his gun to get near us we'll dare ;
We'll scent his vile powder a field-breadth awa',
And soar oot o' danger—caw-caw, caw-caw !

Caw ! caw ! the soft winds blaw,
And melt in the valleys the drifted snaw ;
The boulders appear on the heathery law,
And pickings are plenty—caw-caw, caw-caw !

And who are yon strangers that feasting roam
At the water's edge on the flood-filled holm,
Wi' their green-tinted feathers and crests so braw?
The spring-bringing peesweeps—caw-caw, caw-caw!

Caw! caw! let's cheerily caw;
The children are shouting, "Your nest's awa'!"
The horse through the stubble the plough can draw,
And pickings are plenty—caw-caw, caw-caw!

The sheep on the meadows beheld with delight
The hastening awa' o' the blinding white;
Nae mair they stand scraping wi' weary paw,
But nibble 'mang plenty—caw-caw, caw-caw!

Caw! caw! in concert caw;
The starling shall join us—the laverock, the daw;
And the snipes in the marshes their whistles shall blaw,
For pickings are plenty—caw-caw, caw-caw!

And see the white buds on yon lown willow twig;
Our mates are to woo and their nests are to big;
But that's a sweet toil that fa's lightly on twa,
When pickings are plenty—caw-caw, caw-caw !

SONG—LET US DREAM TOGETHER.

Come, let us dream thegither, May,
　　There's nought so sweet as dreaming;
The joys that purest are on earth
　　Are those that live in seeming.
On yonder bank twa hawthorns spread,
　　Whose buds are kissing ither;
The burn we'll wade, and in their shade
　　We'll sit and dream thegither.

To weave a wreath ye'll gowans pu',
　　And while the stems ye're plaitin',
Delights owre pure for ither een
　　We'll see before us waiting:

And while wi' fragrant rustling down

    The boughs shall lean to screen us,

We, cheek to cheek, owre blithe to speak,

    Shall dream ae dream between us.

ROBIN O' RAPLOCH.

A BALLAD.

PART I.

Young Robin o' Raploch gaed south to the muir,
Wi' his faither's auld gun, and his dog so rare—
A leave or a licence he hadna, I wat,
But Robin o' Raploch cared naething for that.

"What deil wi' a licence want I?" quoth he—
"The hills and the heather to all are free;
Nae leave will I beg for, yet whare is the loon
Daur claim the muir-hen that my gun shall bring down?"

Young Robin o' Raploch had roamed a' day,
And keeper or watcher had crossed nae his way;

He ne'er frae the muir had sae laden gane hame,
For his dog had been keen, and unerring his aim.

By a wee merry burnie he sat down to dine,
Nae roast could he boast o', nor sparkling wine;
Some cakes and a flask frae his pouches brang he,
And Robin was proud as a king could be.

His table he spread on the bent sae lang,
His grace was a stave o' a hunting sang,
Nae guest had he but his dog sae rare,
But Robin o' Raploch dined cheerily there.

But feastin' and happy they hadna been lang,
Till up frae his green couch the auld dog sprang,
And a growl deep and low let his master ken
That foes were approaching, both dogs and men.

Robin o' Raploch sprang fast to his feet,
But he thocht nae o' fleein', though nane were sae fleet;
He grasped his gun when their four foes he spied,
And whispered to Hero—"Keep close to my side."

But vain was his caution, for e'en as he spoke
There burst from the foemen one puff o' white smoke,
And Hero leapt up wi' a sharp howl o' pain,
And dropt ne'er to rise from the green bent again.

But once at poor Hero paused Robin to look;
All fettering emotion he from his heart shook,
And quickly a ball in each barrel he thrust,
While deeply by everything evil he cursed;

And then at the mongrels, that, fierce for the fray,
Tore straining the leash a few paces away,
An instant aimed grimly, then, hit in the head,
The brutes at the feet of the keepers fell dead.

But careless o' that, on the keepers came fast:
" Ah, Robin !" they cried, " we hae found ye at last.
Come, march to the Sheriff, but first to the Ha'—
Yield, Robin o' Raploch, ye're but ane to twa."

Robin o' Raploch was six feet three,
His answer was only a glance o' his e'e ;

His gun on the bent by his Hero he flang,
And slowly he faulded his arms so lang.

But white were his cheek and his lips, I trow,
And wild was the flash o' his een sae blue :
" Gin ye were twenty—and ye are but twa—
Robin o' Raploch would scorn ye a'."

Wi' a fearsome shout, at the twa he sprang,
And his heavy nieves on their breasts he brang—
Twa dreadfu' thuds, and a deathlike mane,
And Robin o' Raploch stood up alane.

Then steevely he bound them back to back,
And syne in a tauntin' tone he spak'—
" Robin o' Raploch's a rare prize to win,
Strike boldly, and tak' him—ye're twa to ane.

" But why should I spare ye, ye cowards," he cried,
" That spared nae the faithfu' auld dog at my side?"
Wi' his een flashin' madly aboon them he stood,
For the Tempter was whispering—" Blood for blood."

G

"Na, na!" murmured Robin, "a taunt or a blow
Till now I ne'er had for a conquered foe;
But nane human blood at my door e'er shall lay;"
And he turned to the bank where his Hero lay.

Sadly he down by his faithfu' freen knelt,
And fondly the pulseless breast he felt:
He strokit its head o' the silken jet,
And his rough brown cheek wi' a tear was wet.

He taen oot his knife, aye sae bright and keen,
And cut out a sod o' the bent sae green;
In the soft damp moss he a little grave made,
And soon owre his Hero the green turf laid.

And aye as he thought o' the dog sae dear,
The Tempter was whispering revenge in his ear:
And oft his brow darkened, his cheek grew mair wan,
And oft the keen edge o' his knife he fan'.

But "Vengeance!" still "Vengeance!" the Tempter
cried:
See! Robin bounds owre to his helpless foes' side,

His foot on them presses, his knife gleams in air,
When the cry of a maiden is heard on the muir.

Half bent o'er his victims stood Robin, and gazed,
His foot on the nearest, his hand o'er them raised,
He stood like a statue, grim, awful, and grand,
The "Vengeance Arrested" of some master-hand.

And then looking round him, uncertain he seemed
If all that had passed was not fancied or dreamed,
Till the maiden's soft hand on his shoulder was laid,
And "Robin! oh, Robin!" she gently said.

Feebly and skaithless his arm fell down,
And the shame-flush spread owre his face sae brown,
And, blending wi' pity, love shone in her e'e,
As "Robin," she murmured, "oh, what's this I see?"

He pressed and he kissed her wee haun' sae white,
And his blue een filled wi' a safter light,
His knife through the bonds o' the keepers he drew,
Then gleaming afar frae his hand it flew.

His gun owre an auld oak root he bent,
In pieces asunder his game-bag he rent,
His powder-flask 'neath his heel crushed he,
And smiled on the ruin so mournfully;

And then turning round wi' a smileless despair,
"Sweet May, o' thy love I need never dream mair;
I'm ta'en, and my future a bairn may divine,
But, May, I would rather been prisoner o' thine.

"A prison, a trial, a trip owre the sea,
Or maybe the gallows, sweet May, waits on me,
For but for thy comin' my haun' would been red,
And the heather been tinted wi' murdered men's bluid.

"As life dear was freedom ae short hour sin syne,
Now life I wi' freedom would careless resign.
Lead on to the Sheriff, since sae it maun be;
Dear May, never mair shall I wander wi' thee."

"Lead on to the Sheriff?" the keepers replied;
"Na, Robin, we'll lea' ye at bonny May's side,

We'll dare the laird's wrath, and ill-luck may he hae
That seeks a rude haun' on your shouther to lay."

Then frae the stained heather their dead lifted they,
And slowly and silent and sad marched away,
And by Hero's green grave lingered Robin and May,
Till the thin gloamin' mist o'er the muir gathered grey.

PART II.

Whare Clyde like a crescent gleamed round a green
    haugh,
Wi' dark woodlands skirted, and bounded wi' saugh,
Whare a rill through the haugh ran wi' saft ceaseless
    sang,
And the grass, green and plenty, thrave a' the year lang,

There close by the wood a trig cottage was seen,
Its roof thatched wi' heather, its wa's ivied green,
And there wi' her grannie 'bade bonny May Lee—
Her grey reverend grannie o' sixty-and-three.

And near the Haugh cottage stood Robin and May:
" Fareweel, May," said Robin, " and maybe for aye;
The laird will be wild when he hears I'm yet free,
And I for my madness maun answer or flee:

" Thy love is the ae sunny spot in my fate,
But how for my comin' can I bid ye wait ?
Fareweel, May, my angel, sin sae it maun be,
I'll face nae the scorn o' your grannie's grey e'e."

" Come in wi' me, Robin; my grannie is kin',
And never says nay to a wise wish o' mine;
I'll tell how you're changed, ye shall plead at my side,
And, Robin, we little ken what may betide."

They reached the Haugh cottage and softly stepped ben.
" Wha's this wi' ye, lassie ? I surely should ken."
" It's Robin," said May; " he was owre on the muir,
And cam' at my seekin' to see how you fare."

Up rose the grey grannie o' sixty-and-three,
And stood like a queen wi' command in her e'e.

" Come owre to my side, thoughtless hizzie," said she ;
" What wants Poacher Robin wi' auld Grannie Lee ?"

" I've come, Grannie Lee, e'en to plead my ain cause,
And tell ye I'm weary o' breakin' the laws ;
The Robin ye kent has departed for aye,
Unworthy was he o' yer ain peerless May.

" But I, Grannie Lee, hae nae dog and nae gun,
And the angel he lo'ed I hae courted and won.
Forget him, he'll ne'er cross your hallan again,
And tell me ye'll gie me your May for my ain."

" The Robin I kent had your face and your e'e,
A braw buirdly chiel, but a worthless, was he ;
Wi' ane that's sae like him my bairn ill would fare—
Let that be your answer, and fash me nae mair."

" Oh, Grannie," pled May, " when the lang nichts hae
      come,
And the storm, loud and eerie, roars down the spence
      lum,

If Robin were wi' us nae bogles we'd fear,
And the black-maskit thieves would nae mair venture
    here."

" Alack ! pleads the lamb for the vile reivin' tod!
'Twere better, my bairn, to be laid 'neath the sod.
The lark wi' the starling may mate on the lea,
But Robin o' Raploch is nae mate for thee.

" Fie, Robin ! nae wonder your cheek blushing burns:
Nae wonder your e'e frae an auld woman's turns !
O' a' but my Marian's ae bairn I'm bereft,
Why seek ye to blight the ae flower I hae left ? "

" I seek nae to blight your ae flower, Grannie Lee,
But would to her aye as the summer sun be.
Lang, lang I hae lo'ed her—oh, Grannie, be kin',
Fu' little ye wist o' the sorrow that's mine.

"My Hero lies cauld 'neath the bent on the muir,
My gun and my flask bow'd and broken lie there;

I'm nae mair a poacher—I've sworn't, and I swear—
And peacefu' and thrifty I fain would bide here."

" This house, Robin Raploch, yon cow and kail-yard,
Yon green rentless haugh, are the gift o' the laird ;
But frae me a' this would his angry haun' sweep,
Should Robin o' Raploch ance 'neath my roof sleep.

" And, Robin, ye ken I am feeble and auld,
And canna weel warstle wi' hunger and cauld,
And sae, if ye hae nae a heart o' the airn,
Ye'll lea' me in peace wi' my bairn's only bairn."

Sad Robin o' Raploch turned roun' on his heel :
" Fareweel, May, my angel—and, Grannie, fareweel;
I'll steal away saftly, the laird ne'er shall ken"—
When wha but the laird, wi' a smile, steppit ben ?

" The laird kens already, bold Robin," quoth he,
" But fear nae. I'll plead for him too, Grannie Lee.
He shall work at the ha'—I've a cow yet to spare,
And May will be surety he'll never poach mair."

INNOVATION.

A DREAM.

WHEN violets were on the hills,
And meadow-queen beside the rills,
While foxgloves decked the moorland dykes,
And bees were busy wi' their bykes,
And lassies thrang amang the hay,
I wandered out one summer day.
And musing—as became a bard—
Like one that neither saw nor heard,
I reached at length the Hyndog Glen,*
It little matters how or when.
There nature revels in the grand,
And welcome on her face I fand;

---

* A beautiful and romantic glen in the hills above Dalry, free to
all wanderers.

She seemed to say, " Come, take a seat,
The flowers shall bloom among your feet,
And ye shall sit on flowers, and flowers
Above ye in their bosky bowers
Shall on you breathe, and birds shall sing,
And butterflies, on rainbow wing,
Shall flit about and seem to say,
' Be cheerful : life is but a day.'

" And if ye sit till tunefu' even,
The glen shall hae the hue of heaven ;
The setting sun frae Beadland braes,
Shall fill the glen with golden haze.
The Rye shall seem a golden stream,
Each sunward leaf with gold shall gleam,
And sweetly indistinct the hum
Of voices from yon bank shall come,
Where bairns in many-coloured duds,
Out-tinting e'en the autumn woods,
The strawberries among are seen,
The straggling rows of briers between,

With cheeks that rival in their hue,
The peerless wildings that they pu'."

I sat not, but, my aimless dream
Resuming, left the glen and stream,
And upward clamb till, ere I kent,
I waded deep 'mang Beadland's bent,
And heard the plover piping loud,
And gazed on Goatfell's cap of cloud,
And marked wi' fancy-glamoured e'e
The heaving of the distant sea.

And to my fancy-quickened ear
The plash at Ailsa's foot seemed near;
I saw, with awe, the mystic line,
Where in the sky the sea we tyne,
And, dimly, Carrick's classic coast,
And Ayr, of Coila's Burns the boast;
And turned with pride a look to steal,
At Swinderidge Muir, where gallant Neil
Roamed often, dreaming of the strife
And glory of the soldier's life,

And haply prescient of tho fame
That now endears his honoured name.

Grown drowsy, down myself I laid,
And o'er my face my napkin spread,
And soon in careless slumber fell,
And dreamed, as I shall shortly tell.

Across the moor twa dames I saw,
Wi' stately step together draw ;
The youngest frae the eastward prest,
The eldest frae the gleaming west.

The last appeared a matron, sage,
And weel aboon tho middle age ;
Her face was pale and something long,
Sonorous was her voice, and strong.
Severely reverend was her air,
And grey her een and grey her hair ;
Her robe o' black behind her trailed,
And she was unco lingle-tailed.

The ither was a dame, I ween,

Who five-and-thirty years had seen ;

Her garments had a modern air,

A velvet net confined her hair ;

Her shapely head had that upon it,

Which modern fashion names a bonnet.

A hoop she wore whose gracefu' swell

Became her sonsy shoulders well.;

Her gown was of the wincey, grey,

And trimmed with velvet gravely gay ;

A silver thistle brooch she wore,

And owre her arm a plaid she bore.

Her een were of the speedwell's hue,

And something sparkling in their blue

Of strength in noble purpose spoke,

And scorn of superstitious yoke ;

And eke a spark of humour keen,

But genial, in their glance was seen.

Whene'er a pleasant thing she said,

About her cheeks two dimples played,

As if uncertain where to stay,
Then passed, when silence came, away.
Unmoved she had an air of sadness,
But laughed the very soul of gladness.

She smiled and spoke.   " Weel met," quoth she
" Our judge and jury ye shall be ;
We here hae come wi' solemn ettle,
A question great and grave to settle."

" Wi' pride," quoth I ; " but may I speir
What unco matter brings ye here ? "
When spoke the eldest, " Wait a wee ; "
Then wi' a measuring stare at me,
" Read ye the papers, sir ? " quoth she.
I answered, " Antrin anes I see."
" The Scotsman ? "   " Yes."   " The Saturday ? "
Quoth I, " Whene'er it comes my way."
Again she pierced me wi' her een,
Until it seemed my thoughts were seen,
Then muttered, " Sinfu' human natur' : "
And something like, " An Innovator ; "

Then added bravely, " Be it sae,
For right is sure to win the day."

" The question that disturbs the nation,"
She then resumed, " is INNOVATION;
And, sir, it's best the truth to tell
At ance—the question's ' Heaven or Hell.'
And ye'll, I beg, keep that before ye
The while ye listen to my story.

" Since ye the ribald ' Scotsman' read,
And if ' The Saturday' ye heed,
I e'en maun tell ye to your face,
I fear ye hae prejudged my case.
But ye at least this truth maun ken,
That, lately, erring sons of men
Their fathers' decent ways forsakin',
And after modern notions traikin',
In spite of fleechin', threatenin', threepin',
By them that hae their souls in keepin',
Like silly sheep are gaun astray,
Nor see that ruin's in their way.

Already, sir, they're at the brink o't,
I'm cauld wi' horror when I think o't.

"O Scotland! hae I seen the day
When ye in kirks can sit and pray,
And there, irreverend, on yer feet
Wi' psalms your Lord and Master greet,
And calmly on a pastor look
Wha reads his prayer frae a book?
And mair and waur—oh, fifty waurs,
To think o't wha wi' patience daurs?—
Within the House o' God they've brought
(There's desecration in the thought!)
A whistle-kist, that, gaily gilt,
And near the holy pu'pit built,
Hauds up its head wi' shameless front,
Defyin' righteous axe and lunt;
And when the psalm for praise is gi'en,
A fiddler chiel, that sits unseen,
Weel hidden wi' a board or screen,
Wi' feet and fingers fuglin' plays
Some rant that modern saints ca' praise;

While a' the congregation staun',
The Book of Books in every haun',
Yet, to the ongaun listenin' mute,
God's praise to gilded pipes depute,
And think their duty done.   My plea
Is that it's sinfu'—what say ye ?"

I summoned reverence to my aid,
And thought, but nought in answer said.

The younger smiled ; " That cuckoo sang,"
Quoth she, " has been her owre-word lang.
She thinks our good and zealous sires
Hae a' escaped the infernal fires,
And chant in heaven's blest dominion,
And that, Sir, is my ain opinion.
But she insists the sons maun ape
Their fathers if they would escape ;
In short, her system of salvation
Consists of reverend imitation,
And proof of virtue lies alone
In gesture, attitude, and tone ;

And here sae widely differ we,
I doubt if we shall e'er agree.

" Deliver standing your petition,
She cries, or your reward's perdition.
To repetitions dreech and dreary
Attend till every leg is weary—
Till strong men shift frae foot to foot,
And inly wish 'twas right to sit :
Or groan, impatient in their pain,
' Lord will he never reach Amen ?'
And some ae desperate step advance,
And sit them down and tak' their chance,
Until a gladsome rustling drowns
The lang-drawn prayer's closin' sounds :
'Twas so our fathers did, and so
Maun we, or wail and gnash below.
" And so in all things else, salvation
Is won alone by imitation.
Our worthy fathers sat and sang
God's praise, and therefore stannin's wrang.

Nae organ, touched wi' faultless skill,
Wi' holy sounds the kirk might fill ;
    And so the hymn—I mean nae jest—
Was but a medley at the best.
They sang, 'tis true, wi' zeal thegither,
But didna wait on ane anither ;
The echoes of the holy places,
Ashamed to hear them, hid their faces ;
Or screamin' to the riggin' flew
As soon's the opening line was through.

" The learned precentor vainly led,
Wi' sic a choir his skill fell dead,
And every ither verse the tune
    He closed himsel', a bar behin' ;
Or, sweatin', noted as he sang
That half the kirk were singing wrang—
The ' Martyrs ' some, and some the ' Bangor.'
What then—was that a cause of anger ?
If half the kirk but kent ae tune,
'Twas surely wise to sing that ane.

Sic things to ony modern ear
Would seem, to say the least o't, queer;
But so our fathers did, and we,
Like them, maun murder melody,
Assured we praise the Lord, in danger
If jarring discord's kept a stranger.

" I say the growin' innovation
Will be a credit to the nation."

" 'Tis ever thus," the elder cried;
" I'm answered aye wi' sneers and pride.
It's wrang to answer fools wi' folly,
And chiefly sae in matters holy,
Else I might answer jeer for jeer—
But what would that avail us here?

" Let it be granted that to sit
At prayers proves amended wit;
And granted, on the other haun',
That at our praises we should staun';

What follows then?   Shall it be said
God maist approves the praise that's played?
If harmony our worship hallows,
What then?   Need it be blawn by bellows?

" Oh! for an angel's arm to sweep
The pests into the mighty deep,
And to simplicity restore
Our worship as it was of yore,
When psalmody was void of art,
Except the warbling frae the heart,
And angels pleased came half-way down
Frae heaven to meet the gratefu' soun'.

" But pleasant are the paths o' sinnin' :
Observe how small was the beginnin',
And note how rapid was the gain of
The ills that I sae sair complain of :—
A pastor troubled wi' the ailin'
Of eild, and findin' memory failin',
And these as good excuses pleadin',
Instead of preachin' takes to readin';

The thing, like Popery's sel', is hated,
But for his sake is tolerated.
A younger pastor hears o't syne,
And thinks he might in readin' shine—
So reads: the people grumble sair,
But then he's placed, they hardly dare
For sic a trifle to disgrace him,
Or ask the synod to displace him.
Another, on some vain pretence,
Of which the root is indolence,
Wi' written screeds his hearers doses,
And turns the leaves before their noses.
And so the innovation grew,
Till now our preachers are but few,
And affhaun' pu'pit declamation
Will soon be lost unto the nation.

" And so in singin' ; ane first brang
A music-fork, and made it twang
Aloud before the astonished people,
Wha could hae hung him frae the steeple—

But, waes me! didna: then ane saw
That if he had a voice or twa
To help alang a kittle air,
'Twad ease him o' a load o' care.
Still swelled the gathering evil higher,
Till each precentor had his choir;
The choir established firm and sure,
The canker then was past a' cure;
And noo our souls the organ vexes,
And what is comin' next perplexes.
What's next? It's easy guessed. Alas!
Alang the laft a band o' brass,
Wi' tinklin' thingumbobs o' steel,
Will help alang the service weel,
And, waes me! nane will in them see
The damning toys of Mammonric.

" The spate at first but swells the rills,
And then the river-banks it fills,
And then, o'erwhelmin' fast the strath,
It roars wi' ruin in its path.

"Say, then, if foolish are my fears,
And say, should I be soothed wi' sneers?"

The ither laughed: "That band of brass
Is good," she said, "and weel may pass
For argument, but I would fain
Convince you that your fears are vain.

"The organ's roll and swell ascending,
Wi' human voices sweetly blending,
In sacred song, ne'er fails to fill
Wi' such emotions as should fill
The soul that worships; but the blare
Of brazen bands were coarser fare,
And few will entertain the notion
Of sic assistants to devotion.
Confess your fears were mere pretence,
Unworthy of a douce defence,
And only in your kindness mooted
That it wi' ease might be refuted.
The ither phases of the 'canker'
(The term is yours), I canna hanker

Wi' merry haun' to brush awa',
Convinced that whare ye thocht ye saw
A festerin' and a deadly wound,
. The part is healthy, hale, and sound;
There's naething in the choir to fear—
And say, which would ye rather hear?
A pastor hankerin' owre his text,
By treacherous memory sair perplexed,
Wi' stammerin', stutterin', and repeatin',
Affronted, and wi' torture sweatin',
Yet flounderin' on wi' zeal profound,
Tae fill the alloted hour wi' sound:
Or ane that brings his 'written screed,'
As ye would ca't, affhaun' to read—
Why should the turnin' o' a leaf
Be cause of anger or of grief?
Since frae the harvest of his meanin'
The flock may carry hame a gleanin'.

" Shall none but those whose angel tongues
Frae far can charm delighted throngs—

Like Guthrie, or Macleod, or Caird,
Or Candlish—be wi' patience heard?
Would ye the nation's pu'pit close ·
To all but those and such as those?
The river of majestic thought
That flows upon their tongues unsought,
Delights us only here and there,
And's not expected everywhere.

"And why should printed prayers distress?
Think you their influence is less?
If they to memory were committed,
The scrup'lous conscience might be suited;
But where the difference would be,
I frankly own I fail to see.

"Oh! wherefore should we walls erect
To keep asunder sect from sect?
Why should I think my narrow road
The only path that leads to God?
And, looking proudly o'er my wall,
Think all but me in Satan's thrall?

And, like the Pharisee of old,
All virtue in myself behold?
And speak as if the entrance-fee
To heaven were Christian liberty?
Oh! sister, we the walls must raze
That hem us in our narrow ways;
And less exclusive texts employ,
Whose use-in-chief is to annoy ;
And practise less our lair and wit,
On hairs of doctrine trebly split ;
Nor ire provoke, with keen contention,
On things above our comprehension.
And charity our rule maun be,
Till Christian intercourse is free.
One aim we have, one faith, one God ;
Oh ! sister, let us walk one road !
Be this our task—' One Christian Union ;'
And this our motto—' One Communion ;'
And when the nickname ' sect' 's deleted,
We'll rest and think our work completed.
Oh ! let our senseless bickering cease,
And let us jog to heaven in peace."

Then smiling, and with hand extended,
Quoth she, " I trust our quarrel's ended."

The elder curtsied, and with pride
Replied, "The umpire shall decide."

How I got up wi' solemn hem !
And ca'd my hearers " Miss " and " Mem,"
And wi' confounding eloquence,
And deep-convincing common sense,
Confuted this, and that admitted,
And this ane praised, and that ane twitted,
Until the elder's sel' began
To say " There's something in the man,"
Some ither pen than mine maun tell—
It's doubtfu' praise that praises sel' ;
But thus I ended—" Sisters, ye
Maun gi'e the kiss of peace, and 'gree;"
And, haith, nae sooner had I said it,
Than, smiling, they advanced and did it.
I saw their een wi' joy were gleaming,
And then I woke, and had been dreaming.

ASPIRATION.

" Oh ! father, we read in the schoolroom to-day
Some lines that from memory will not pass away;
And they've caused in my heart such a pleasing sing-
  song,
I've done nothing but think of them all the day long :
No sum would come right, and how stupid I felt
When the master had marked all the words I misspelt.
I was forced with my long-cherished medal to part;
But less than the ode my disgrace fills my heart.
And yet there seems nought to make any one sing,
For the verses were all about cuckoos and spring.
What's poetry, father ? (for, doubtless, you know),
And whence the strange power of its jingle and
  flow ?"

" Ah ! boy, you your father's poor wisdom o'ertask—
No mortal can answer the questions you ask ;
Some say, ' 'Tis the sweetest words happily waled ;'
And some, ' 'Tis where rhyme has o'er reason prevailed.'
In grammar you find it reduced to a rule,
But it is not a thing to be learned at the school :
The source of its power long a mystery has been,
And, here, it will aye be a mystery, I ween.
Great minds full of learning to solve it have striven,
But it baffles them still, like the star blaze of heaven."

" And where did it come from ?"

       " Some say from above,
The first gift to man from the Father of Love.
The one deathless pleasure that flits o'er the earth—
In human emotions it daily has birth :
'Tis it that gives sadness to sorrow's wild wail ;
'Tis it that gives gladness to mirth's happy hail.
To thrill a pleased world it from peace emanates ;
It shouts on the war-fields of mad human hates.
On the flower-hills of heaven to revel it soars,
And regions where stars have not ventured explores.

Now a bird calls it forth, now a bud, now a flower ;
Now gloaming awakes it—now dawns holy hour ;
Now it hangs o'er a dewdrop, now floats on a river,
And·all that it touches is sacred for ever."

" What wonder this wakens ! but surely I've heard
That poetry's only the voice of a bard,
Or the tones of a harp.—Is it so, father ?   Well,
In what happy land do the harper-bards dwell ?"

" In all lands, my son.   In the city they're found,
And out in the country ; on hills ; under ground.
They croon in the hut by the wild souching sea,
And in the old cot 'neath the lone moorland tree.
Some live by their song, while the world wonders how ;
Some pine at the shuttle, some follow the plough ;
Some sweat at the forge, and some bend o'er the awl—
They dream in the palace, the manse, and the hall :
For the spirit that whispers, ' Thy lot is to sing,'
Now speaks to a peasant, and now to a king."

"Oh! father, how much I am longing to sing
But one ode like that of 'the cuckoo and spring;
I long 'mong the singers of earth to be heard,
And when I am old to be hailed as a bard;
For, doubtless, on everything pleasant they fare,
And are of their countries the pride and the care."

"Ah, no! silly boy, they are nobody's care,
And they must, as they can, on life's pleasant things
    fare.
A few have with Fortune tript on as they sung,
But many have wandered life's sorrows among;
Yet singing so well that the world oft declared
Their song grew the grander the harder they fared.
They spring, like the coltsfoot, where men least ex-
    pect,
And seldom droop chilled by the blight of neglect.
In the hardest of lots they find something that's sweet;
They stoop and lift beauties at common men's feet.
With hope in the future, and joy in the past,
They sing, as the lark warbles, facing the blast."

I

" And what good do they do ?"

" You may ask me as well
What good does the blackbird that sings in the dell,
Or the violet that blooms on the brow of the hill,
Or the music that lives in the linn-leaping rill :
They brighten our lives, and they lighten our cares,
But the bard has a mission far nobler than theirs.
To him human language its beauty all owes—
The graces of virtue 'tis his to disclose ;
And Liberty's stay on the earth he prolongs,
For tyranny fears less the sword than his songs.
Let bards and their poetry bid us farewell,
And men would be demons, and earth would be hell."

" Are they happy and wise, father ?"

" Tuts ! how you ask !
Why should you the wit of your father o'ertask ?
There are people who say—but perhaps say amiss—
' The bard's but a finger-post pointing to bliss.'
' Poor fellow,' say others, ' his wit's taken wing ;
But his business is not to be wise, but to sing.
His sayings with sound are so sweetly relieved,

Their lack of sound wisdom is little perceived.

He's not very stable, but prone to do wrong,

But we pardon him much for the sake of his song—

And singing, you know, is a simple affair,

He has only to think of some old happy air,

And look at the sky with his chin lifted—so,.

And his words of themselves in sweet measure will flow.

If e'er he goes fishing for thoughts, he's at fault,

For the thought that is angled for's never worth salt.'

So lightly, my son, of his wisdom talk men,

And he justifies all that they say now and then.

" Myself have seen one standing still, like a fool,

In the rain, at the brink of a little road-pool,

There weaving the first happy lines of a strain,

Whose burden (to be) was ' The beautiful rain ; '

What music its low measured pattering awoke,

And to those who would listen how wisely it spoke !

How it scorned in the clouds to be longer confined,

And to reach the dull earth made a steed of the wind ;

How it paused in its flight the bare hedge to adorn,

By hanging a pearl on the point of each thorn ;

How it trickled down trees in the tiniest rills,
Or gathered in torrents to rush from the hills ;
How it came when it chose, not at any one's call,
And meant no offence in its falling at all.

" But the wise ones of earth might have envied the
    fool,
Who stood so entranced by the little road-pool—
Not fearing the storm nor complaining of fate,
He smiled like an angler on Garnock in spate.
He was craving an alms at the threshold of thought,
And took with delight the poor pittance he sought.

" The rain-drops were mortals, the little pool earth,
And the bubble each drop made at falling was birth,
And the circle that spread round each drop when it fell,
To the mark a man makes in the world answered well ;
And the meeting and breaking of circles the strife
Of men jostling men in the battle of life ;
Though the bubbles and circles to some might reveal
The bob and the whirl of a blithe Scottish reel,

That memory would waken, and make the cheeks glow
With the music and dancing of long years ago.

" In the brattling of burns, and the glistening of leaves,
The Bard more than others aye hears and perceives ;
The mountain afar, through the mist peering dim,
Is more than a vapour-veiled mountain to him.
Dear, dear is the glen where the green ivy creeps,
And the beech-bough the face of the mossy crag sweeps;
And, oh ! how delicious the vague gloaming dream,
Where the fern-royal's dipping her fronds in the
        stream—
How dear the delight when he stealthily roams
In the wood's sacred shade where the great river foams ;
For inanimate things, that to others are mute,
For.him have a voice and a cheerful salute."

" How grandly your words on my wondering ears fall !
But, father, their meaning comes not at my call :
That bards should hear ought in the voice of the
        stream,
Beyond a sweet murmur, a marvel doth seem ;

Why flowers in their presence should cease to be dumb,

And mountains ought else than great mountains become,   .

Seems more than a wonder—but why it is so,

I fear is not meant that a schoolboy should know.

Sometimes as I walk from the school all alone,

I smile when I think what a dreamer I've grown;

And once—more than once, father, many a time—

I've wondered to find myself thinking in rhyme,

And wondered still more when á thought, ere I wist,

Would start into view like a ship in the mist,

And startle me strangely, and then, ere I knew,

Like a ship in the mist it would flit from my view;

And often I've found my tears ready to fall,

When the phantom thought would not return at my
call.

And now I've but one wish, and that is, to sing

Just one ode like that of the cuckoo and spring."

A STRUGGLE.

Oh ! wherefore tempt me thus, sweet Muse ?
  Why on me smile so kind and fainly ?
Though ever dear as summer dews,
    Alas ! I dare not entertain thee ;
I'm captive in the realms of lair,
And have for thee no fitting fare.

Oh ! wherefore tempt me thus ?   Thou art
  No more a solace nor a pleasure ;
With thee, once mistress of my heart,
    For dalliance now there comes no leisure ;
To rhyme, that once such pleasure gave,
I am no more a willing slave.

With book and rocks surrounded, see
  My drooping fancy, wae and wingless,

Sits fondling with dejected air
    The harp she fears will soon be stringless ;
While Hope, of sunny dreamland queen,
Sits in the shadows of the scene.

Still dost thou smile ?   What wouldst thou sing
    If I with wonted warmth should press thee ?
Of love, or care, or odorous spring,
    Whose zephyrs all, unthanked, caress thee ?
Ourselves ?   Poor Muse ! can it be so ;
Art thou reduced to themes so low ?

Nay, nay, I know thou canst not brook
    The heart that yields a half devotion,
Nor swells, if thou but deign'st to look,
    Up in a spring-tide of emotion.
What canst thou have for him but hate,
Who, e'er he sings, must calculate ?

Farewell, farewell ! I dare not trust
    My longing hand in thine, sweet charmer ;

Fools only warfare wage with must—
    I dare not, if I would be warmer;
Nor stop to ask if we do wrong
To part, who have been friends so long.

I must not pause to ask if, when
    The crawbell from the grass is peeping,
And in the flowery stream-thrilled glen
    The blackbird's heart to love is leaping,
There shall be power in human art,
Sweet Muse, to keep us then apart.

When from the thorn the first fair spray
    Of bursting blossom-buds I'm pu'ing,
Must I still wish thee far away,
    The gathering swell of song subduing,
And hear the rapture of the lark,
Without a note my joy to mark?

Shall I the early primrose see,
    So sweetly with its leaves contrasting,

And round the sloe-bloom hear the bee,

    While yet the breeze that bloom seems blasting,

And pass as if I cared not, lest

My thought in song should be expressed?

Oh! why is it so sweet to sing?

    Oh! Muse, why dost thou smile so brightly,

And meanly stoop thy pearls to fling

    Before a fool that rates them lightly?

With thee a drag in learning's race,

My only prize must be disgrace.

ELEGY

AND are ye dead, my braw black cat,
That was sae sleekit aye and fat !
Your fur was aye like John's new hat
      When brushed fu' tentie,
And muckle praise your beauty gat
      Frae a' that kent ye.

May ne'er guid-luck be near the gamie
That aimed your hurt, my gleg kin' Tammie,
And made your skin sae cauld and clammy,
      Wi's cursèd slugs ;
For ye were gentle as a lammie,
      And worth ten dowgs.

What though he met ye in the wud,
Whare scores o' feckless rabbits whud ?
He needna grudged ye ae puir fud
     O' lawfu' prey.
Oh, may his gun, wi' thriftless thud,
       Shoot aye agley !

Puir Tam ! I'm sure we'll miss ye sair;
It's just sax years come Glasgow Fair
Since ye brang in your first young hare—
     A fat wee thing ;
For ye were ane that aye took care
       The best to bring.

Ye ne'er would learn to fetch and carry,
Nor e'er to jump owre hauns would tarry,
But weel ye lo'ed to hunt and harry
     When nicht had lowered;
Then, licht o' foot as ony fairy,
       The woods ye scoured.

Nac hidden stamp e'er hurt your paw,
Nae deadly bait e'er crossed your maw,
But wi' a snuff o' scorn ye saw
        Their poisoned flesh;
For, lion-like, ye likit a'
        Your feasts ta'en fresh.

Nae mice alive your nose e'er passed,
And when ye had them hard and fast,
Up in the air ye would them cast,
        And kep benignly;
And though ye swallowed them at last,
        'Twas aye done kindly.

That winter when the lang frost lay,
When John gaed idle mony a day,
Ye were amaist our only stay—
        The Lord was wi' ye;
Though John wad never let me say
        He held ocht to ye.

Ye mony a dainty hare brang in,
Some warm, and wi' nae broken skin:
The heads, it's true, o' mair than ane
      We never saw,
But wi' a gratefu' look aboon
      We used them a'.

Ae nicht—I'll min't for evermore—
(Grim want cam' in the nicht before,
And to refill our empty store
      Nae south wind cam')—
A something scartit at the door;
      Quo' I, "That's Tam."

And to the door in haste I flew;
And when ye in your burden drew,
I fand my heart come to my mou'
      Wi' gratefu' swell;
And dearer frae that hour ye grew,
      Than's wise to tell.

We read hoo, by a lonely brook,
Weel hidden in some rocky nook,
A prophet frae twa ravens took
      His Heaven-sent fare,
While they their glossy plumage shook
      And flew for mair.

But mony a time, when ye brang in
Your prizes wi' sae little din,
I thocht (it was a fearfu' sin,
      And showed my havins)
Ye had the angel 'neath your skin
      That led thae ravens.

Sic sense as thine is rare, I trow;
Ye kent, I kenna why or hoo,
Whare safety frae your claws was due
      To bird or beast;
For though ye o' a stranger doo
      Hae made a feast,

Yet when oor hens wi' chickens gaun
Were temptin' ye on every haun',
Ye on your paws would let them staun',
      And sangs has sung them,
When ony ither cat wad fa'en
      Like fire among them.

Oh ! muckle are we in your debt !
For friens like you are rarely met;
Death never says, " If ye'll regret
      I will not strike,"
But flings his dart, and lets us fret
      As lang's we like.

Ye were a brute o' noblest kind—
I had amaist said " noblest mind "—
For in ye I could naething find
      To meanness swerved.
Some are the human rank assigned
      That less deserve't.

The happy glimmer o' your e'e,
Auld Tam, I never mair shall see,·
As when your wee drap ream and tea
        Ye daily gat;
Nae venison to you could be
          Sae sweet as that.

The sang o' birds the woods within,
The poet's praise ne'er fails to win
(It lifts his soul the world aboon,
        And sweetens thocht),
But to the music o' your croon
          Their sang was nocht.

You, sleepin' soundly on my lap,
My apron never mair shall hap—
To sweeten your bit morning nap
        Was aye my care ;
Nae kindly word or kindly clap
          Can cheer ye mair.

K

But, Tammie, ye shall live in sonnet;
John o' your skin would mak' a bonnet,
Your snout and paws he would hae on it,
   A show to see !
But I will wad a groat, and won it,
    That ne'er shall be.

In honouring ye we baith shall vie,
And we a braw glass case will buy,
Whare your trig form, fu' warm and dry
    And clean, we'll keep,
And ye upon my drawers shall lie,
    And seem asleep.

JEAN TAMSON'S DREAM.

YESTREEN I dreamed a dream, John—a kirk I thought
 mysel',
Wi' lichened wa's and dumpy tower, and old familiar
 bell;
And raws o' flowering trees—the thorn, the chestnut,
 plane, and lime—
Kept bees aboot me bummin' aye through a' the summer-time.

And high upon a hill I stood, whare a' the parish
 saw—
My very station seemed to prove my right to read the
 law;
And there was nae excuse for them that by me dared to
 steer,
For I had but to wag my tongue to let the parish hear.

But though a kirk I seemed, John, o' sturdy lime and
stane,
I thought the power that wrought the change had little
frae me ta'en ;
For I could hear, and see, and smile, and shake a
friendly haun',
And, thumpin' strongly in my breast, I fand my heart
aye gaun.

Nae mortal e'er had sic a dream ; for as I gazed aroun',
And let my e'e frae fragrant dells pass owre the busy
toun,
I saw amang the slaty waste, as sure as sure could be,
Yoursel', that nae disguise could hide, a kirk as weel as
me.

And wi' your old ambition, John, that nae misluck e'er
tired,
E'en to my height upon the hill I thought ye had aspired ;
Aboon the highest lums I saw your vane had mounted far,
And in the moonbeams faintly shone beside the laigh-
most star.

But, John, I thought ye seemed sae trim, sae freshly
    scoured and gay,
Sae lacked the douce decorum that a kirk should ever
    hae,
That sorrow gathered in my heart, and wandered to my
    e'e,
And we, I thought, were pairted, John, together ne'er
    to be.

I kenna how it cam' aboot, but, someway, as I gazed,
The veil that hid your secret thoughts by some fell
    haun' was raised,
And sic a sight ! They were nae thoughts that in a
    kirk should dwell,
And that which seemed the thought-in-chief was how
    to help yersel'.

I couldnae trust my senses, and I seemed aboot to drap
Wi' loathing, and I hid my een and farther frae ye crap;
And when again I lookit, as my heart wi' pity glowed,
A river broad and ferryless I thought between us rowed.

I gazed upon the foamin' flood in wonderment and awe,
And, oh ! the angry words I heard were waur than a' I
    saw ;
Your curses, clothed in saintly terms, cam' surgin' owre
    the stream—
It maun hae been the Fiend himsel' that banned me in
    my dream.

And as I gazed frae hill and dale, frae hamlet, ha', and
    toun,
A great unreckoned multitude was gathering fast aroun';
And had ye been an angel, o' the joys o' heaven wha sung,
Nae louder shouts o' triumph could amang the hills hae
    rung.

And aye as ye misca'd me, John (oh, this was warst ava !)
Amang the mad applauding crowd my ain dear bairns
    I saw ;
They forward wi' the foremost pressed, and yelled, and
    hissed, and groaned,
And would, had Heaven permitted, me, their reverend
    mother, stoned.

And aye ye patronage denounced, and raved o' martyrs'
blood,
And like a prophet reamin' fou o' inspiration stood :
Sae glib your gab, sae hard your cheek, your power o'
prayer sae great,
It seemed as if ye had a voice in the affairs of Fate.

Oh, surely ne'er were spitefu' words to human ears sae
sweet !
For muckle was the treasure they were pourin' at your
feet ;
I couldnae keep frae thinkin' o' the fools o' ancient days,
Wha brang their wealth, a gouden calf, at Horeb's feet
to raise.

'Twas pitifu' to hear ye whiles my comin' doom bewail,
And fearfu' was your thunder when the funds began to
fail ;
But chief your wheedling powers excelled, sae sweet
your coaxing smile,
Ye frae the craw wad wiled the egg, had it been worth
your while.

Ah! John, it was a fearfu' dream—I far mysel'
forgat,

And when ye "kettle" cried, sometimes would weakly
answer "pat."

I thought nae o' the fatted calf, and wished ye care and
skaith,

And claimed and revelled in the glebe that might hae
sair'd us baith.

It was a weary facht we focht, and far we baith gaed
wrang—

We cared nae how we soiled oursels if dirt we only
flang;

And aye in ither's cares we saw the haun' o' angry
Fate—

It's humbling to believe twa kirks could hate wi' sic a
hate.

It's true I fand the tears at times cam' drappin' frae my
een,

When for the needfu's sake your plans were mair than
ord'nar' mean—

Forgettin' that nae cottar thrives wha scorns to use
the rake,
And them that by their wits maun live, maun keep
their wits awake.

But, John, before I wauken't a sweet change cam' owre
my dream—
We baith forgot to rail, and then less darkly flowed the
stream
That rowed between us, and I gazed and saw it narrow-
ing, till
It murmured at our feet a bright and gently murmuring
rill.

And better far than that, I thought my hand ye kindly
ta'en,
And blessed me wi' the kiss o' peace that made us ane
again ;
And just when angels hovering near wi' harps and
palms I saw,
I wauken't wi' a start, and fand we ne'er were kirks ava.

TO MRS H. WILSON.

DEAR MADAM,—

I hae been your debtor
In that important thing—a letter.
How lang?   'Twill be a month gin Monday;
I thocht to write ye every Sunday.
(Hae patience; here we're in the mirk,
And hardly think aboot the kirk.)
But by the nichts and weeks aye slippit,
And my resolves in bud were nippit;
But noo a canty screed I'll gi'e ye,
And surely patience will be wi' ye.
Between my lugs I hear a hummin',
Nae human skill can guess what's comin';
And just as little could it guess,
If 'twill be common sense, or less;

But you, I trust, o' this are sure,
It can at best be naething mair.

· · · · ·

Dec. 21.

Dear Madam, I had weel intended
My letter should yestreen been ended ;
But when wi' muckle toil I got
My Hobby spurred into a trot,
As fate would hae't, the youngest wean,
Seized sudden wi' some inward pain,
Began to greet, and grat sae lang
And sair, that by my pen I flang.
For though my muse, when in the mood,
Can in a Fair find solitude, .
And to the close would croon her strain,
She canna bear a greetin' wean.
So to the promise that was gi'en,
Anent a canty screed yestreen,
Ye maunna haud me, else I fear
A sorry strain ye're like to hear,

For the puir bee within my head
Is either stiff wi' cauld, or dead ;
If it should prove to be the latter,
There's nocht, I think, would please me better,
For mony a weary tramp it's cost me,
And mony a bonny penny lost me.
Oh, Jove! in anger ye decreed it—
Why should a collier be bee-headed?
Oh, keep that madness 'mang the gentry,
Wha cash and leisure hae in plenty,
And far frae ane whase toils and groans
Maun keep his weans in duds and scones.

Some speak about the boundless pleasure
O' croonin' sonnets at your leisure,
Or croonin' when wi' heavy wark
The sweat is steamin' frae the sark.
Alas ! the pleasure's but a flash—
True pleasure bides wi' nae sic trash.
It's true, that when to new-spun rhyme
The ringin' pick is keepin' time,

The weary shearin's sooner shorn,
And labour's burden lichtly borne;
But hardly hae we sung our sang,
Till wi' our worldly cares we're thrang—
For, sneer about it as we will,
The world's our lord and master still.

He only has on earth a heaven,
To whom the gift divine is given
Of livin' only for the hour;
He never sees misfortune lower.
Does want draw near?   He hears nae tell o't.
Despair?   He ne'er endures the hell o't.
Though penniless, he's never puir
(True wealth is only want o' care).
But ane sae highly blest, I fear,
Can hardly hae existence here;
If ane there were, vile human nature
Would scorn to trust the happy creature.

Alas! that we should be sae fear't
For ills that end, and aye sae sweer't

To think that, though a cloud hangs o'er us,
A happy sunshine waits before us.
Why nurse despair, the serpent guest
That stings the hospitable breast?
They say the bairn that's ance been brunt
Has aye a fear o' fire and lunt.
Is this, when we are auld, the reason,
That hope's sae aften oot o' season?
Oh, sweet is faith! but still the fact is
We fear the bitter pill o' practice,
And fail to mark the "silver linin'"
O' clouds that keep the sun frae shinin'!

What think ye?   Write and say.   Adieu!
Ye'll gi'e my best respects to Hugh,
And say 'twill be my pride and pleasure
To ca' as soon as I hae leisure.

Yours,

D. W.

ABRAHAM.

WHAT is the cry that comes
  O'er the blue main,
Wrathfully, wailingly?—
  "Abraham's slain!"
Abraham, the honest, slain!
  Can it be true?
Has he been venturing
  Where battle-balls flew?
Aiding a circle
  To close round the foe,
And urging the soldier
  To strike the last blow,
And there, as a soldier would,
  Sudden laid low?

Ah! not as soldiers would
  Draw the last breath;

Ah ! not as citizens
　　Fain would meet death ;
Not on the rutted plain,
Cresting a mound of slain,
Straining his dying ear
Victory's voice to hear,
Pleased if he hears it
　　Swell faintly afar ;
Not in a weeping home,
Waiting till doom would come,
Cheered by Love's presence
　　And Hope's bright'ning star.
While in the house of glee,
Founding a jubilee,
Smiling and happy he
　　Loyal eyes fed :
E'en while a grinning clown
Wooed noisy plaudits down,
Sudden a hidden hand
　　Death's message sped—
Sudden the martyr's crown
　　Dropped on his head.

What will men say of him?
What dare they say,
But that an honest soul's
Hurried away?

Hearken!—Some after him
Shouting, thus cry—
"Spirit of Abraham,
Where wouldst thou fly?
Wouldst thou to heaven ascend?
Dar'st thou to grace pretend?—
Hitherward, spirit, wend;
Leave not the land,
Till of a nation's blood
Washed is thy hand.
Pass o'er each battle-scene;
Float where the torch has been;
Pause where the widows sigh;
Look in the orphan's eye:
Then of the saints on high
Join the bright band;

L

Dare 'mong the chosen then,
    Spirit, to stand."
What do men say of him?
    Thus they dare say—

" Earth had no tyrant
    Like him that's away :
Heartless and gaunt and grim,
Why should we weep for him?

" Was he not loathingly
    Friend of the slave?
Was it not grudgingly
    Freedom he gave—
Never beholding
    Their chains till pressed hard,
Then using their sinews
    As sharpers a card?

" What for their scourgings
    And groanings cared he?
What on his ribald lips
    Meant liberty?

Not a deliverance
From long-suffered ill,
But only permission
To plunder and kill.

" He, when he cried to them,
'Lo, ye are free !
No longer black cattle
But citizens ye,'
But meant his sweet sayings
And smiles broad and bland
Would ruin and rapine
Spread o'er a fair land.
Weep for him? Weep for a
Tyrant that's gone ?
May every tear shed for him
Burn to the bone !"—
Thus of the soul away
Ruined men dare to say.

Wail, lyres, your saddest tones ;
Mourn, Afric's sable sons—

That which he did for you
  Was not his all.
Had he been spared to you,
More had he dared for you ;
Hard has he fared for you,
  Mourn for his fall.
Europe, speak well of him,
All the good tell of him,
Letting his short-fallings
  With his heart rest.
He in a tangled web
Wove with a knotted thread,
Doing what mortal
  Could do for the best.

Abram the Honest's gone,
Struck from the people's throne ;
Well may they sigh and moan,
  'Bating their glee,
Sounding a note of woe,
E'en while the conquered foe,

Yielding, unwilling, low
  Bends the proud knee—
For where hath Columbia
  Better than he?

THE BIRDIE.

I MET a wee bird in the early dawn,
　　When the morning star was shining,
That hovering aboon me said, " Whare are ye gaun,
　　Your morning slumber tyneing ?"

" I'm gaun to yon cliff wi' the broomy brow,
　　With the linn beyond it leaping,
To sit and gaze on the pool below,
　　With peace in its bosom sleeping.

" I'm gaun to gaze on the tranquil pool,
　　While the star-decked east is brightening,
To dream of the ending of sorrow's rule,
　　And labour's burden lightening."

" What sorrows hae ye ?" said the little bird,
　Its dark e'e kindly beaming,
" And what is the labour that leans so hard,
　And tints wi' grief your dreaming ?

" Why come ye on tempting cliffs to mope,
　In the dark pool's peace believing ?
I fear you've been listening to flattering Hope,
　And bear like a bairn her deceiving."

" Oh ! little ye ken, bonnie bird," I said,
　" The strength of a human longing,
When sleep-reiving cares on a ruthless raid
　Are round his pillow thronging ;

" And little ye ken how he longs for peace,
　When the future gives no token
That the bark of life will from heaving cease
　Till the anchor-chain is broken.

" Ye hae nae been fretting 'neath sorrow's rule,
　Nor vigils with care been keeping,

And ken nae how sweet is the tranquil pool,
  Wi' peace in its bosom sleeping."

"Gang hame to your bairns," said the little bird,
  "And the wife that waits and wearies,
And blush if nae sweeter thoughts are stirred
  By the glee o' your lisping dearies.

"Gang hame to your bairns," said the scornful bird,
  "And as you're hameward faring,
Observe the poor in yon rows that herd,
  Your lot with theirs comparing.

"There children in squalid rags you'll meet,
  The breath of Boreas scorning,
While leaving the print of their naked feet
  In the snow of the winter morning;

"And Hope with their fathers and mothers has been,
  With tales of bliss deceiving;
But none on yon tempting cliff are seen,
  In the dark pool's peace believing."

" And what are their troubles, O bird ! to me,
　But danger-beacons burning?
I fear them as landsmen fear at sea
　The weathered gale's returning.

" I saw in the starlight a shadow gaunt,
　And as the day grows clearer,
I fear 'tis the form of the giant Want
　That's slowly drawing nearer:

" I knew him of old, and I fear his rule—
　How grandly the linn is leaping !—
Sweet bird, let me pass to the tranquil pool,
　With peace in its bosom sleeping."

So on to the cliff with the brow of broom,
　The tortuous path I wended,
And me far up in the " scattering gloom "
　The little bird attended.

But the linn now fell with a sullen roar,
　That seemed of the angry ocean,

And the once still pool was trembling o'er
With an eerily-glimmering motion.

There Peace, no more like a spirit bright,
Me down to her breast seemed wooing;
But a writing in fire was the ripple-light,
And the written word was " Ruin."

THE SIN O' SANG.

I'VE come, sweet Jean, while owre the hills
   The evening shadows steal—
I've come to give thee back thy love,
   And say for aye, fareweel:
It is nae that my love's grown cauld—
   For that can never be;
But I hae sinned the sin o' sang,
   And daurnae wed with thee.

I thought my dreams were " beams frae heaven,"
   And hailed them aye wi' glee;
For aft they showed a happy home,
   Whare thou the queen should be.

And Hope was ever at my side,
  New pleasures to reveal ;
And so I sinned the sin o' sang,
  And I maun say fareweel.

Oh ! dinna look sae waefu', Jean ;
  Nae heartless loon am I,
To win a bonny lassie's love,
  Then careless bid good-bye.
Oh ! fondly, fondly I hae wished
  To win thee for my ain ;
But I hae sinned the sin o' sang,
  And now maun wed wi' nane.

To him who sins that deadly sin,
  And canna frae't refrain,
Thrift's sure to be the rainbow's base,
  Pursued for aye in vain.
Oh ! seldom will they drink o' joy,
  Who life's cup wi' him pree,
And, Jeannie, I hae sinned that sin,
  And daurnae wed wi' thee.

Oh ! had I but in secret sung,
   And won nae praise but thine,
A lot that angels might hae grudged,
   Dear Jeannie, would been mine.
But, far and near, the're some that ken,
   And my reward is sure—
A loveless and a lonely home,
   And eke a life o' care.

Oh ! if there had been but one hope
   To shimmer in the van
Of labour's battle, I for thee
   Would fouchten like a man;
And like a man I'll fight, although
   Success will smile nae mair;
For I hae sinned the sin o' sang,
   And maun for aye be puir.

Thou kens that in the hive o' life
   No idler I hae been,
But aye wi' glowing hands amang
   The toilers hae been seen;

But "This is he that murdered Time"
Is written on my brow,
And wha in a' the busy world
Will dare to trust me now?

TO COUNCILLOR WILSON,

GLASGOW.

February 23, 1863.

DEAR SIR,—

THANKS for the printed speech ye sent me.*

In ryme I fain would compliment ye,

But faith my muse has grown so lame

O' ryme, I scarce can mind the name,

And wi' a blush I e'en maun tell't,

I've clean forgot the way to spell't.

I ken an "h" should be in ryme,

For I hae written't mony a time,

But whether it should follow "y"

Or "r," uncertain now am I.

---

* Referring to a speech of which he sent me a copy.

But owre the thing I didna swither.
Quo' I, " I'll out wi't athegither—
What matter when I hae the soun'?"
And sae the " h "-less ryme gaed down.
When next I use't I'll make it right,
But I maun be excused to-night.

But yet, sir, I maun compliment ye :
It is a charmin' Bab ye've sent me ;
Sae tastefully it's tied thegither,
But few could tie me sic anither.
On sic a Bab, and sic a string,
What muse could gaze wi' faulded wing ?
For months I hae nae felt sic pleasure.
Oh ! for an hour o' quiet leisure,
That I micht sit and let the fire
O' Burns's muse my soul inspire
Until (as aft before) I'd feel
As if I at his feet did kneel,
And felt his haun' upon my head,
And saw his mantle owre me spread—

His dark e'e kindly on me beam,
The star o' an eternal dream.

But, while I write, frae roof tae hallan's
Like bedlam wi' thae noisy callans :
O' a' the Deils wi' which we're curst,
The Printer's Deil's by far the worst ;
But his allotted place he fills,
Like other necessary ills.
(Be't understood, dear sir, whate'er
I say o' him he maunna hear.
He needs be neither dumb nor blate
Wha meddles wi' the Fourth Estate,
And soon or late he'll sure sink under
Some weel-aimed bolt o' morning thunder.
Sae wi' the inky imp my plan
Is aye to praise him when I can.)
At times, when fancy lacks employment,
His din's a source o' true enjoyment;
But though he aften plagues me sair,
To wish him ill were hardly fair.

M

There is a kind o' fellow-feelin'
That owre my heart at times comes stealin':
I mind how I in youth was cuffed
Like him, when I my maister huffed,
And how, the less I would oppose,
The thicker cam' the ungenerous blows;
I sabbed, 'tis true, in piteous mood,
But he! it seems to dae him guid.

There's no 'tween coal and printer's ink
Sae muckle odds as ane wad think;
Indeed, we may the difference split
Between the pressroom and the pit:
They hae the din, I had the damp;
They hae their gas, I had my lamp;
My toil the sunlicht never saw,
And theirs the sunlicht sleeps awa';
And though they're aye the earth aboon,
I had the Country, they the Toun.

I said we micht the difference split
Between the pressroom and the pit,

But as I on comparin' gang,
In sooth ! I think the sayin' wrang ;
A bairn o' mine, however dear,
I'd rather see him there than here.
O' " Life " he aiblins less micht learn,
But he wad langer be a bairn,
Micht leeve a life a thocht mair sainted,
His tongue wi' filthy slang less tainted.
Alas ! to hear them ane wad think
The verra earth ashamed wad sink ;
O' vilest deeds they tak' the credit,
And say wi' shameless front, " I did it ;"
Remarks that they think only smart,
On wrinkled cheeks gar blushes start.
Sae learned in the affairs o' woman,
God help us ! they appear scarce human.
The beardless rakes ! O death ! be kin',
And keep frae that ilk bairn o' mine.

And sae, sir (though I've far digressed),
What wi' their rampin' and unrest,

Their rattling, clattering, deaving din
(The devils a' wear wooden shoon),
A guid new thought that's worth rehearsin'
Can ne'er be putten decent verse in,
And ane in prose his say maun sum,
Or listen fretfu' and be dumb.

There was a time, it's no lang gane,
And owre't 'twere hardly wise to mane,
When I had but to say, I'll sing,
And straight my ready muse took wing.
Stiff was the theme! she rose the prouder!
Loud was the noise! she sang the louder!
Like prisoned laverock in the town,
That strives the causeway din to drown;
But now the Dame is grown sae taupit,
She maun be coaxed, and praised, and clappit,
And maunna be disturbed, or she
Will mute as winter blackbird be,
Else I in Burns's praise wad join
And tie a Bab to eke to thine.

And yet, dear sir, what can we say
That would be new ?   For mony a day
Enthusiasts in his praise hae sung,
And commentators sage hae wrung,
Frae every line its subtlest meaning :—
There's little left for future gleaning.

Ca' we him Scotland's ain—her best !
It is a truth by a' confest.
Great master o' the Doric reed !
It is a praise that's stale indeed.
The pride o' every honest man !
For sixty years the strain's sae ran :
Though sonnet follows sonnet fast,
Yet each but counterfeits the last,
And that which tells his praises best
Seems mair an echo than the rest.

His memory lang within my heart
Has been a star that " dwelt apart ;"
But of its ever-growing beams
To sing, to me irreverend seems.

I dare not to a theme aspire,
That seems too grand for human lyre.

Again, sir, let me compliment ye
On the rich paper ye hae sent me.
This random rhyme ('tis weel spelt noo)
Is but a puir return, 'tis true,
And doubtless it wad been far better
That I had still remained your debtor,
Than sic vile payment sent—but then,
As soon as I had ta'en my pen,
My thoughts in measured form cam' clinkin',
Wi' every thought a rhyme cam' linkin',
And sae I wrote awa, ne'er heedin'   .
If what I wrote was worth the readin',
Till decency I far owrestep't it,
But, sir, in lieu o' thanks accept it;
You see in rhyme I'm prone to sin yet,
Good-bye,

                    Your Servant,

                         DAVID WINGATE.

W. WILSON, Esq.

OCTOBER—THE GREEN HILLSIDE.

A song for dun October,
  That tints the woods wi' broon,
And fills wi' pensive rustling
  The wooded dells aroun',
While lintie, merle, and mavis
  Nae langer pipe wi' pride,
Nor larks wi' song salute us
  On the green hillside.
Auld nests are noo beginning
  To peep frae woods fast thinning,
And, wi' nae thocht o' sinning,
  Lairds death are scatterin' wide ;
While some are grumblin' sairly,
  O' fields that yield but sparely ;
But nature yet looks rarely   .
  On the green hillside.

What though our posie borders
  In waefu' plight are seen—
Though stocks and staring dahlias
  Hae tint their summer sheen ?
Thy hoary dawns, October,
  They ne'er were meant to bide,
Unlike the halesome clover
  On the green hillside.
Though Robin's town-notes swelling,
  O' summer's flight are telling,
A sober thought compelling,
  That nane would seek to hide ;
Shall we at hame sit chaunnering,
  O' frost and famine maundering,
While wiser folks are wandering
  On the green hillside ?

We'll see the souchin' peesweeps,
  In gatherin' flocks prepared
To leave the glen and meadows,
  Whare love's delights they shared ;

Their cheerfu' cries we hear nae,
    As owre our heads they glide.
Poor birds ! they part in silence
    Wi' the green hillside.
And though nae lambkin's gambols
    May cheer us on our rambles,
O' hips, and haws, and brambles,*
    Ilk brake we'll reive wi' pride,
And pu' the lingering gowan,
    Whare, late, the clustered rowan,
In scarlet grandeur glowin',
    Graced the green hillside.

When streams the gouden sunset
    Frae 'tween the hills and cl'uds,
While hangs the double rainbow
    Aboon the sparkling woods,
In the herald lull that tells us
    The storm-king by will ride,
Oh ! wha would haste in terror
    Frae the green hillside ?

* Hips, haws, and brambles—wild berries.

What though the clouds close o'er us,
And glens grow dark before us,
Some bush frae blustering Boreas,
Will ample beil' provide,
While thoughts we lang shall treasure,
The bairns o' purest pleasure,
Shall leap in canty measure
On the green hillside.

Oh ye wha life are wearin'
Amid the city's smeek,
It's no in noisy taverns
Ye pleasure's face should seek.
'Mang " social tankards foamin',"
She cares nae lang to bide,
But weel she lo'es the freshness
O' the green hillside.
For summer's flight she cares nae,
And winter's frown she fears nae ;
To slight poor toil she dares nae,
Nor frae him seeks to hide.

By burnies murmuring sweetly,
   At morn or e'en she'll meet ye,
And wi' a smile will greet ye,
   On the green hillside.

THE CHIELD OOT O' WARK.

SOME tell hoo the turtle-doo mourns for its mate,
Some tell hoo puir Peggy laments faithless Pate,
Some muses mak' wan hopeless widows their mark;
But wha cares a snuff for the chield oot o' wark?
We hear o' the sodgers in battle that fa',
We hear o' the sailors that waves wash awa',
In ballads they'll sing o' their lost bonny bark;
But wha mak's a sang o' the chield oot o' wark?

The chield oot o' wark disappointment maun bear,
Maun suffer wealth's frown and its cauld heartless sneer;
Ilk sumph o' a gaffer may mak' a wit-mark—
A butt for his scorn o' the chield oot o' wark.
He wanders aboot frae dull morn to grey e'en;
Where'er Hope invites him, he's sure to be seen;

But aften Hope's star dwindles doon to a spark,
And hides frae the e'e o' the chield oot o' wark.

The chield oot o' wark, see ! his guttas are dune,
His breeks are threadbare, an' his coat's wearin' thin ;
And though he can brag yet o' mair than ae sark,
How long will't be sae wi' the chield oot o' wark ?
His wardrobe maun gang to the sharks o' the pawn,
For backs maun be bared at the belly's commaun' :
He'll soon hae sma' need to be learned like a clark,
Wha values the gear o' the chield oot o' wark.

His wee things at hame—but o' them speir nae mair—
Their weal is his comfort, their misery his care ;
Their wants wauken thochts unco sinfu' an' dark,
That whisper relief to the chield oot o' wark.
Nae honour for him, let him tramp as he may—
He mauna aspire to the laurel or bay ;
And nae smiling Queen prins a bright hero-mark,
To shine on the breast o' the chield oot o' wark.

The chield oot o' wark mauna beg—daurna steal,
An' pride bids him struggle his grief to conceal:
Believe me, my friends, since the days o' the Ark
The dreif wretch on earth was the chield oot o' wark.
Ye wealthy, on whom wit and wisdom descend,
Oh ! be it your care him frae want to defend ;
On Fame's deathless page he may scribble his mark,
Wha plans a relief for the chield oot o' wark.

A RAMBLE.

WHILE gloaming grey on dell and brae
　Wi' dripping wing is settling doun,
Beside the flowers o' yesterday
　I set me doon a sang to croon.
Wi' happy friends I climb again
　The whinny knowes sae blithely ranged,
And wi' them pu', wi' heart fu' fain,
　Thae floral gems sae sadly changed.

Frae hazel bower to steal that flower
　Wi' emerald leaf and gouden cup,
Through scroggy gill, by tricklin' rill,
　Wi' boyhood's glee we scramble up.
Our feet are on the hallowed hills,
　Whare bards hae strayed and heroes striven ;

The hymn o' streams and laverocks seems
An echo o' the hymn o' heaven.

What joy to hear the tit-larks near,
    In slae-thorn brake whare nane we see,
Whare linties chant, and goldies haunt,
    And hermit foxgloves feast the bee ;
Though blossomed hawthorns are nae seen,
    Nor trees festooned wi' woodbine sweet,
Here's lady's-mantle gouden-green,
    And balmy thyme blooms 'mang our feet.

Wi' gratefu' e'e mouse-peas we see
    Adorn the dykes wi' tufts o' blue ;
Wi' mosses rare, and speedwells fair,
    And gracefu' ferns, our hauns are fu'.
Wha says that we're wi' slavery cursed ?
    It is nae true—it ne'er was true ;
When flowers sae fair auld Nature nursed,
    They ne'er were meant for slaves to pu'.

And noo our downward course we wend—
   The loch's in view ! the loch's in view !
The waters gleam ! the heron's scream
   Comes harsh the hazy distance through.
Amang yon knowes, through mazy links,
   The Lavern glides wi' dimpling smile,
Syne owre the braes, wi' hasty jinks,
   Trips blithely wimpling doun to toil.

See Raggit Robin owre the bent,
   His bonnet waves in rosy pride ;
Has Flora for our pleasure sprent
   The balmy, breezy, cool loch-side ?
See, as the ripple shoreward streams,
   And moves the reeds wi' gentle lave,
Each distant wave a sea-bird seems,
   Each distant floating bird a wave !

N

THE BETTER LAND.

" COME ben and tak' the muckle chair, the wife's at
 Wishaw toun ;
Fu' blithe she'll be to see ye, and the 'bus will bring
 her doun.
Sit doun and warm your feet, and thowe the cranreugh
 frae your hair ;
I fear ye shouldnae venture out in sic a frosty air.

" The bottle's toom ; but, Geordie, Jean has ta'en the
 jar awa',
And, to gi'e you the hans'ling o't, the cork she'll blithely
 draw ;

I seldom fash wi't noo—indeed, I swore I ne'er wad
  pree,
But Jeanie whiles insists, and draps a cinder in my tea.

" And so, till she comes hame, we'll fill our pipes and
  tak' our smoke,
And crack o' times awa,' when we bore lichtly labour's
  yoke—
When hearts were light and bluid was warm, and short
  the blithesome year—
When mist and frost, and rain and win', were faced
  without a fear."

" Ay, Willie, we are turnin' auld and frail; for me,
  I'm done,
My picks beneath the bed ha'e lain unused sin' sixty-
  ane ;
My auld pit-breeks this mornin' wi' the ragman gaed
  on tramp,
And Peggy for a scourin' thing's hung up my auld
  pit-lamp.

"I'm sure I neednae keep my picks nae mair than keep
    my claes—
An auld and weel-worn collier, Will, I maun be a' my
    days;
Sweert's, sweert's my breath to come and gang, and
    whiles it seems to swither,
And wonder if it were nae best to leave me a'the-
    gither.

" Whiles, Will, I dover in my chair, and muse on days
    awa',
When Peg and me were young, and had nae backs to
    cleed but twa—
How hard I wrocht, what sprees I had (for I was fool-
    ish then),
And thocht (if e'er I thocht) the aim o' life was ' won
    and spen'.'

"My Peggy hain't as weel's she could, and wrocht
    whene'er she micht,
And muckle flate, and weel advised, and strave to keep
    me richt.

I ne'er would own't, but weel I kent 'twas wrang—and
    unco wrang :
But what's the guid o' frettin' owre a thing that's by
    sae lang ?

" When roun' me whiles I look and see the plenishin'
    we hae—
A meal for every mornin', and a hap for every day —
And think ' Whase guidin's this?' man, Will, a mist
    comes owre my e'e ;
There never was a better wife, sin' wives began to be.

" She minds it yet.   Teth ! ay, she minds't, and
    mentions't noo and then,
When neebor wives come in to bann their idle,
    drunken men.
But even then wi' kindly clasp she tak's my pithless
    haun',
And whispers, ' Gude be thankit, ye were ne'er a lazy
    man.'

"It's perfit true! I likit wark, and blithely at it sang,

My verra pick was proud o' me, and while I wröcht it
    rang;

There's joy in drinkin'! even in stauns (if short) there's
    wealth o' mirth,

But nocht's sae sweet as weel-paid wark amang the joys
    o' earth.

" Ah, Will! when stauns tak' place, we sit amang the
    chiefs nae mair;

Ye never hear them cryin' nóo, 'Put Geordie in the
    chair!'

But ance I was an oracle, and crowds o' men could
    charm;

I needed but to lift my voice and wave abreed my arm.

" Ah, man! It was a triumph aye to see in print my
    name,

And ken that ' Geordie's ' words were read a thousand
    miles frae hame;

And hear the fules o' editors denounce me for a rogue,

A stirrer-up o' strife—a pest—a wanderin' demagogue.

"I likit it ! but, Will, thae days are frae us ever gane;
The wark we had to do is done, and a' our say is sain;
We noo maun turn our een to things that ance were
    reckoned nocht,
And mair about 'the Better Land' maun think than
    ance we thocht.

"Our Missioner, an honest man, wha jokes a harmless
    joke,
And has a humble heart, and likes a hamely crack and
    smoke, . .
And has a hope for a', and has nae fearsome tale to tell
O' weepin' and o' wailin' in the lampless pit o' hell—

"He says that in 'the Better Land' there's food and
    raiment aye,
And noble drink that rins in burns, and naething for't
    to pay;
Nor rent, nor stent, nor heavy darg, to cross its borders
    dare,
And collier, master, lord, and laird, are equal-aqual
    there.

"Nae asthma's there, wi' weáry wheeze, to wear the
    life awa',

Nor rheumatism, Will, for there there are nae banes to
    gnaw;

Bereavement comes nae there to clip Affection's cord in
    twain,

And Discord's voice is never heard in a' the wide
    domain.

"We'll soom about on wings, like doos, and blithesome
    hymns will chant,

Wi' which compared, earth's sweetest airs are yill-
    house roar and rant,

And join wi' fau'tless skill, untaught, some 'Hallelu-
    jah baun','

Or dreamin' sit, on gouden harps to thrum wi' tireless
    haun';

"Or wanderin' owre the sunny hills, 'mang flowers
    that never dee,

We'll crack, and wonder at our lair o' a' we hear and
    see;

And surely, Will, if hearts we hae, they'll warm wi'
  gratefu' glow,
When we the life in heaven compare wi' collier-life
  below.

" And, Will, we hae nae lang to wait—Death soon will
  draw the screen,
And prove the land we dream o' has nae human fancy
  been;
And what we'll dae, or what we'll say, a wonder
  needna be—
That there's a Better Land ava's enough for you and
  me."

NOTES TO ANNIE WEIR.

Page 4 (a)—"Where the rigs are bower yet." *Hower*—Where the strata and soil above the workings of the pit had subsided.

Page 5 (b)—"And up the weary stairs wi' her coal-creel laden." Where the pits were shallow the coals used to be carried by girls and women to the surface. They had a "creel" slung over their shoulders. The road from the bottom to the mouth of the shaft was a series of short stairs. This must have been very hard work.

Page 5 (c)—"In the twilight dim." Even when the sun shone it would be twilight in the shaft, owing to the interception of the light by the woodwork of the stairs.

Page 7 (d)—"Coming ben." Towards the faces is "ben," or "in;" towards the pit bottom from the faces is "but," or "out."

Page 7 (e)—"Frae the waste aroun'." *Waste*—The wrought-out workings of the mine.

Page 8 (f)—"In the shearing I was thrang." *Shearing*—The most advanced part of a working face.

Page 8 (g)—"For it's coming like a blast." Coming like the *blast* caused by an explosion of fire-damp. "She's blastet" is still a common way of saying there has been an explosion in a pit.

Page 8 (h)—"The black and stoury flood," &c. Bearing on its surface the light coal-dust of the mine.

Page 13 (i)—"And, waking, heard what seemed the hum of bees." In reality the hum of innumerable small flies which the rising flood had driven to that part of the mine.

Page 13 (k)—"When the phosphor-light we saw." *Phosphor-light*

—Sometimes over certain kinds of wood-props used in mines there creeps a network of a brown weed, pointed with white.   In the absence of lamp or candle light it emits a faint phosphoric gleam, which when first seen is alarming even to a man of ordinary courage.

Page 15 (*l*)—" Frae another, ebber pit."   *Ebber*—Near the crop-out of the seam.

Page 15 (*m*)—" Three weary days they, hour aboot, had redd." *Redd*—To remove the fallen roof-stones in the mine.

LIST OF SUBSCRIBERS.

Dr Robert Young, Woodville, Chapelhall.
Mr William Russell,   do.
Mr George M. Russell,   do.
Mr Robert Paterson,   do.
John Crum, Esq.,   do.
Mr James Russell, miner,   do.
Mr Thomas Forsyth, do.   do.
Mr James Gibson,   do.   do.
Mr Thomas Paterson, do.   do.
Mr Robert Wilson,   do.   do.
Mr Robert Gibb,   do.   do.
Mr Thomas Gibb,   do.   do.
Mr John Forsyth,   do.   do.
Mr William Yuill, Glasgow.
Thomas Johnston, Esq., Stevenston House, by Holytown.
Mr William Aitken, Stevenston Colliery.
Mr John Dargavel,   do.   do.
Mr George Haldane, Balbardie   do.
Mr Thomas Hair,   do.   do.
Mr Archibald Prentice,   do.   do.
Mr James Adam, miner, do.   do.
Mr Alexander Hamilton, Legbrannock Store, by Holytown.
Mr William Smith, Calderbank Store, by Airdrie.
Mr —— Lauder,   do.   Office,   do.
Mr David Connor,   do.   do.   do.
Mr Hugh Ferguson,   do.   do.   do.

Thomas Morton, Esq., Milton Cottage, Motherwell.
John Craig Waddell, Esq., solicitor, Airdrie.
J. Montgomerie Alston, M.D.   do.   (4 copies).
John Shaw, Esq., clothier, do.
James Hendry, Esq., National Bank,   do.   (2 copies).
James Kidd, Esq., banker,   do.   do.
George Thomson, Esq., do.   do.
Mr John Harvie, druggist,   do.
Mr Thomas Love,   do.
Matthew Waddell, Esq., Newmains,   do.   do.
Robert M. Rodger, Esq., factor, Airdrie (2 copies).
Frederick Penny, Professor of Chemistry, Andersonian University,
    Glasgow.
Mr John Kirkland, Newmains Store, by Wishaw.
Mr William Eadie, Barkip Store, Dalry, Ayrshire.
Mr James Clark, Armadale Colliery, Bathgate.
Mr John Shanks, Glengarnock Store, Ayrshire.
James Baird, Esq.,   do.   Ironworks, do.
Mr John Thomson, Woodhall Office, by Airdrie.
Library, Ardeer Ironworks, Ayrshire.
Mr J. Scobbie, Fortisset Colliery, Shotts.
Mr Andrew Wingate, Mossend Ironworks.
John Pettigrew, Esq., 2 Brougham Terrace, Glasgow.
Andrew Cassels, Esq., merchant, Hamilton.
James Ferguson, Esq., H.M. Customs, Grangemouth.
William Govan, Esq., 15 Renfield Street, Glasgow (2 copies).
William Govan, jun., Esq.,   do.   do.   do.
John Watson, jun., Esq., coalmaster, 123 St Vincent Street, Glas-
    gow (4 copies).
Mr Thomas Brown, 176 Stirling Road, Glasgow.
Mr John G. Couper, 16 Virginia Street,   do.
Mr John Miller,   do.   do.
Mr William Strang,   do.   do.
Mr Thomas Lindsay, jun., 36 St Vincent Place, Glasgow.
Mr Peter Lennox, 49 Maxwell Street,   do.
Mr Francis Braidwood, 12 Argyle Street,   do.
William Shanks, Esq., manager, Omoa Ironworks, by Motherwell.
John Ferguson, Esq.,   do.   (2 copies).

Mr John Dyer, engineer, Omoa Ironworks, by Motherwell.
Mr D. M'Callum,   do.   do.
Hugh Robertson, Esq., Omoa Foundry.
Mr Thomas Thornton,   do.
Mr John Brown, underground oversman, do.
Mr James Watt, Wishaw.
Mr Joseph Waddell, Newarthill.
Mr Thomas Lithgow, Meadowside, Clelland.
Mr Alexander Smith,   do.
Mr James Johnston,   do.
Robert Pettigrew, Esq., Enniskillen, Ireland.
Mr James Anderson, Farme Colliery, Rutherglen.
Moses Park, Esq., Glasgow (2 copies).
William Barrie, Esq., Indian Civil Service, Bengal (10 copies).
Andrew Barrie, M.D., Bombay Medical Service,   do.
Mrs Barrie, Westhouse, Avondale.
Miss Barrie, Newarthill.
John T. Barrie, M.D., do. (25 copies).
William Higgins, Esq., Back o' Moss, Shotts (2 copies).
James Boag, Esq., teacher, Omoa,   do.
Mr James Tennant, shoemaker, Strathaven.
Mr James Radcliffe, colliery manager, Ashton (4 copies).
Mr William Wright, Hamilton (10 copies).
Mr James M'Donald,   do.   do.
Mr William Naismith, do.   do.
Mr John Kay, Motherwell,   do.
Alexander Whammond, Esq., teacher, Hamilton (3 copies).
Mr John Govan, jun., 15 Renfield Street, Glasgow.
Mr William Govan, 44 West Nile Street,   do.
Mr James P. White, Shawlands,   do.
Mr J. Mackeuzie Melville, 14 Nicholson Street, Greenock.
Mr P. M'Crockett, 41 Holmscroft Street,   do.
Mr Charles Mill, 20 Union Street,   do.
Mr James Carmichael, 39 Nicholson Street,   do.
W. J. Marshall, M.D.,   do.
Mr Thomas Kay, 19 Brisbane Street,   do.
Mr John Walker, F. Terrace,   do.
Mr John Browne, 28 Brisbane Street,   do.

Mr Robert Morison, H.M. Customs, Greenock.
Mr Archibald Denniston, writer,   do.
Mr Samuel Duncan, Havelock Buildings, do.
Mr R. Bruce Bell, civil engineer, 4 Bothwell Street, Glasgow.
Mr Daniel Miller,   do.   do.   do.
Mr H. C. Dixon, 7 West Nile Street,   do.
   (2 copies).
Mr John Ballardie, 3 Carlton Place,   do.
   (2 copies).
Mr William Cowan, 172 West George Street,   do.
   (2 copies).
Mr John Neilson, 7 Eldon Place,   do.
   (2 copies).
Mr David Law, 8 West Princes Street,   do.
   (2 copies).
Mr James Easton, 3 Abbotsford Place,   do.
Mr J. B. Fitzroy, 116 Renfrew Street,   do.
Mr William Wighton, 83   do.   do.
Mr John Binnie, 53 Eglinton Street,   .   do.
Mr William Hutchison, 37 Carnarvon Street,   do.
Mr James Hamilton, 27 Apsley Place,   do.
Mr William Skirving, 5 Florence Place,   do.
Mr Malcolm Kerr, 89 Queen Street,   do.
Mr James Richardson,   do.   do.
Robert Gourlay, Esq., Bank of Scotland, Laurieston,   do.
Mr Robert Donaldson, 71 St Vincent Street,   do.
Mr David Sutherland, 88 Pollock Street,   do.
Mr J. B. Mirelees, 45 Scotland Street,   do.
Mr William Tait,   do.   do.
Mr Thomas Newton, Canning Street, Calton,   do.
Mr Colin Campbell, Scotland Street,   do.
Mr James Blair,   do.   do.
Mr William Forbes, Canning Street, Calton,   do.
Mr Robert C. M'Pherson, Scotland Street,   do.
Mr Alexander D. Whitelaw, Sidney Street,   do.
Mr James P. Crawford, 76 Eglinton Street,   do.
Mr William Pollock, 21 St Vincent Street,   do.
   (2 copies).

Mr Duncan Hunter, 60 St Vincent Street, Glasgow.
Pat. Alexander, Esq., A.M., Great King Street, Edinburgh.
James P. Steele, M.D., Edinburgh.
Alexander Smith, Esq., College, do.
Mr Robinson Rigg,   do.
Alfred R. Cattan, M.A.,   do.
James Gardiner, Esq., S.S.C.,   do.
Mr C. Home Douglas,   do.
Mr David Smith,   do.
Mr J. F. M'Lellan,   do.
Mrs Alexander, St Andrews.
Dr Adamson,   do.
Mr John Alexander, do.
Mr Hugh Alexander, do.
Mr Andw. Alexander, do.
Mr Patrick Anderson, Dundee.
Mr Matthew Alexander, Millig's Cottage, Helensburgh.
Mr Hugh Beckett, 11 Buckingham Terrace, Glasgow.
Mr John Sime, Manse, Kilwinning.
Edward Alexander, jun., 43 Campbell Street, Glasgow.
Mr John Alexander,   do.   do. (2 copies).
Mr Walter Alexander, 29 St Vincent Place, do. (4 copies).
Mr John Finlay, 12 Renfield Street, do. (10 copies).
William Wilson, Esq., 42 Glassford Street, do. (20 copies).
Mr Gordon Smith, 133 West George Street, do. (18 copies).
Mr Daniel Macnee, Montague Place, do. (4 copies).
Mr William Cross, 73 Mitchell Street, do. do.
Mr Alexander Harvey, Govanhaugh, do. do.
Mr R. F. Easton, 81 Buchanan Street, do. do.
Alexander Thomson, Esq., architect, 183 West George Street, Glasgow (20 copies).
Mr Andrew Finlay, 5 Buchanan Street, Glasgow (4 copies).
Mr Francis Smith, 27 Sandyford Place, do. do.
James B. Gartly, Esq., 29 St Vincent Place, do. (3 copies).
George T. Gartly, Esq., St Vincent Street, do. (2 copies).
John B. Gartly, Esq., 22 Springfield Court, do. do.
Duncan M'Laurin, Esq., Clydesdale Bank, do. do.
George E. Ewing, Esq., sculptor, do. (4 copies).

o

Thomas Colquhoun, Rousemont House, Helensburgh.
F. H. Thomson, M.D., West George Street, Glasgow (8 copies).
Robert Somers, Esq., 'Morning Journal,'   do.   (5 copies).
John Mossman, Esq., sculptor,   do.   (6 copies).
Mr David M'Cubbin, 93 West Regent Street,   do.   (2 copies).
Mr William Johnston, 70 George Square,   do.   (4 copies).
Mr R. J. Currie, Burton-on-Trent (4 copies).
Mr P. M'Gregor, Lonend House, Paisley (2 copies).
Rev. George Turnbull, Pollockshaws (2 copies).
R. Towers, 18 Woodside Place, Glasgow.
R. Scobie, Airdrie.
A. Allan, Windmillhill.
H. A. Lambeth, 117 Hill Street, Garnet Hill.
Dr W. B. Hamilton, Dalry, Ayrshire.
Dr Archibald Blair,   do.
Mr James Stirrat,   do.
Mr John Gow,   do.
Theop. Paton,   do.
Mr Archibald Cunningham, Eglinton Ironworks.
Mr David Brown, bookseller, Dalry.
Mr Robert Greig,   do.
Mr James M'Kie,   do.
Mr James Stirrat, jun.,   do.
Mr John Kerr,   do.
Captain Crichton, Linn,   do.
Mr William Wallace, Balliol College, Oxford.
Mr John Adamson, High Street, Kinross.
Mr Duncan Adamson, Ben-Rhydding, Leeds (2 copies).
Mr John Paterson, Glencairn Lodge, Motherwell.
Mr A. W. Buchan, 144 West Regent Street, Glasgow.
Mr William Hamilton, 125 Buchanan Street, do.
Mr Thomas S. Hutcheson.
Mr William Campbell, Dunoon.
Mr —— Fulton, engraver, Duke Street, Glasgow.
Dr S. Thomson, Motherwell.
Mr Millin,   do.
James Russell, Esq., do.
Mr George Russell,   do.

Mr William King, Motherwell.
Mr Oliver Summers, do.
Mr Thomas Saunders, do.
Mr George Anderson, do.
Mr T. G. M'Cubbing, Bank of Scotland, Motherwell.
Mr William Shirlaw, City of Glasgow Bank, do.
Mr John Howard M'Lean, Carfin House, do.
Ironworks Library do.
Mr Russell, banker, Coatbridge.
Mr Jack, factor, Dalziel.
Mr William Ker, Motherwell.
Mr J. G. Leadbetter, Hillside, Bothwell.
Mr J. Ferguson, 93 Frederick Street, Glasgow.
Mr James Cuthbert, 7 Kellermont Street, do.
Supt. John Christison, Wishaw.
Mr James Hunter, Glenhead Camp.
Mr William Bell, Bellevue Cottage, Wishaw.
Mr Daniel Rose, Balliol College, Oxford.
Mr G. Todd, do. do.
Mr Henry Craik, do. do.
Mr A. Bell, do. do.
Mr John A. Scott, do. do.
Mr A. Mitchell, Trinity College, do.
Mr Michael Balfour Hutchison, Lincoln College, Oxon.
Mr Richard Wren, Glasgow (2 copies).

THE END.

PRINTED BY WILLIAM BLACKWOOD AND SONS, EDINBURGH.

MESSRS BLACKWOOD AND SONS'

RECENT PUBLICATIONS.

—o—

THE TALES FROM "BLACKWOOD."

A Cheap Re-issue, in Monthly Volumes, at 1s. Volume I. is published.
To be completed in 12 vols.

CORNELIUS O'DOWD UPON MEN AND WOMEN, AND

OTHER THINGS IN GENERAL. Originally published in 'Blackwood's
Magazine.' 2 vols. crown 8vo, 21s.

"The flashes of the author's wit must not blind us to the ripeness of his wisdom, nor the general playfulness of his O'Dowderies allow us to forget the ample evidence that underneath them lurks one of the most earnest and observant spirits of the present time."—*Daily Review.*
" In truth one of the most delightful volumes of personal reminiscence it has ever been our fortune to peruse."—*Globe.*

TONY BUTLER.

Originally published in 'Blackwood's Magazine.' 3 vols. post 8vo, £1,
11s. 6d.

"No novel of the season has given us so much genuine pleasure; and we can with safety predict that every reader will be delighted with it. Skeff Damer, and Tony, and Count M'Caskey, will live in the memory for many a day. They are all three, in their way, perfectly original conceptions and are as true to the life as any portraits ever drawn by pen and ink."—*Standard.*

THE PERPETUAL CURATE.

By the Author of 'Salem Chapel.' Being a New Series of the 'Chronicles of Carlingford.' 3 vols. post 8vo, £1, 11s. 6d.

" We can only repeat the expression of our admiration for a work which bears on every page the evidence of close observation and the keenest insight, united to real dramatic feeling and a style of unusual eloquence and power."—*Westminster Review.*
" The 'Perpetual Curate' is nevertheless one of the best pictures of Clerical Life that has ever been drawn, and it is essentially true."—*The Times.*

FAUST: A DRAMATIC POEM.

By GOETHE. Translated into English Verse by THEODORE MARTIN.
In 1 vol. post 8vo, 6s.

Illustrated Edition of PROFESSOR AYTOUN'S

LAYS OF THE SCOTTISH CAVALIERS.

The Designs by J. NOEL PATON, R.S.A. Engraved on Wood by John
Thompson, W. J. Linton, W. Thomas, J. W. Whymper, J. Cooper, W. T.
Green, Dalziel Brothers, E. Evans, J. Adam, &c. Small 4to, printed on
toned paper, bound in gilt cloth, 21s.

" The artists have excelled themselves in the engravings which they have furnished. Seizing the spirit of Mr Aytoun's 'Ballads' as perhaps none but Scotchmen could have seized it, they have thrown their whole strength into the work with a heartiness which others would do well to imitate. Whoever there may be that does not already know these 'Lays,' we recommend at once to make their acquaintance in this edition, wherein author and artist illustrate each other as kindred spirits should."—*Standard.*

THE DISCOVERY OF THE SOURCE OF THE NILE:

A JOURNAL. By JOHN HANNING SPEKE, Captain H.M. Indian Army. With a Map of Eastern Equatorial Africa by Captain SPEKE; numerous Illustrations, chiefly from Drawings by Captain GRANT; and Portraits, engraved on Steel, of Captains SPEKE and GRANT. 8vo, 21s.

"The volume which Captain Speke has presented to the world possesses more than a geographical interest. It is a monument of perseverance, courage, and temper, displayed under difficulties which have perhaps never been equalled."—*Times.*

WHAT LED TO THE DISCOVERY OF THE NILE

SOURCE. By JOHN HANNING SPEKE, Captain H.M. Indian Army. 8vo, with Maps, &c., 14s.

"Will be read with peculiar interest, as it makes the record of his travels complete, and at the same time heightens, if possible, our admiration of his indomitable perseverance, as well as tact."—*Dispatch.*

A WALK ACROSS AFRICA;

Or, Domestic Scenes from my Nile Journal. By JAMES AUGUSTUS GRANT, Captain H.M. Bengal Army, Fellow and Gold-Medallist of the Royal Geographical Society. 8vo, with Map, 15s.

"Captain Grant's frank, manly, unadorned narrative."—*Daily News.*
"Captain Grant's book will be doubly interesting to those who have read Captain Speke's. He gives, as his special contribution to the story of their three years' walk across Africa, descriptions of birds, beasts, trees, and plants, and all that concerns them, and of domestic scenes throughout the various regions. The book is written in a pleasant, quiet, gentlemanly style, and is characterised by a modest tone. . . . . The whole work is delightful reading."—*Globe.*

STRAY LEAVES FROM AN ARCTIC JOURNAL;

Or, Eighteen Months in the Polar Regions in Search of Sir John Franklin's Expedition in 1850-51. To which is added, THE CAREER, LAST VOYAGE, AND FATE OF CAPTAIN SIR JOHN FRANKLIN. By CAPTAIN SHERARD OSBORN, C.B. A new Edition, in crown 8vo, with a Map, 5s.

CAXTONIANA:

A Series of Essays on LIFE, LITERATURE, and MANNERS. By SIR EDWARD BULWER LYTTON, Bart. 2 vols. crown 8vo, 21s.

"It would be very possible to fill many pages with the wise bright things of these volumes."—*Eclectic.*
"Gems of thought, set upon some of the most important subjects that can engage the attention of men."—*Daily News.*

THE CAIRNGORM MOUNTAINS.

By JOHN HILL BURTON. In crown 8vo, 3s. 6d.

"One of the most complete as well as most lively and intelligent bits of reading that the lover of works of travel has seen for many a day."—*Saturday Review.*

ESSAYS ON SOCIAL SUBJECTS.

From the 'Saturday Review.' Crown 8vo, 7s. 6d. Third Edition.

"In their own way of simple, straightforward reflection upon life, the present century has produced no essays better than these."—*Examiner.*
"We shall welcome the author again if he has more to say on topics which he treats so well."—*Guardian.*

THE SCOT ABROAD,

AND THE ANCIENT LEAGUE WITH FRANCE. By JOHN HILL
BURTON, Author of 'The Book-Hunter,' &c. 2 vols. crown 8vo, in
Roxburghe binding, 15s.

"Mr Burton's lively and interesting 'Scot Abroad,' not the least valuable of his contributions
to the historical literature of his country."—*Quarterly Review.*
"An excellent book, that will interest Englishmen and fascinate Scotchmen."—*Times.*
"No amount of selections, detached at random, can give an adequate idea of the varied and
copious results of reading which are stored up in the compact and pithy pages of 'The Scot
Abroad.'"—*Saturday Review.*
"A charming book."—*Spectator.*

THE GREAT GOVERNING FAMILIES OF ENGLAND.

By J. LANGTON SANFORD and MEREDITH TOWNSEND.
CONTENTS:—The Percies—The Greys of Howick—The Lowthers—
The Vanes or Fanes—The Stanleys of Knowsley—The Grosvenors—The
Fitzwilliams—The Cavendishes—The Bentincks—The Clintons—The
Stanhopes—The Talbots—The Leveson-Gowers—The Pagets—The Man-
ners—The Montagus—The Osbornes—The Fitzroys—The Spencers—The
Grenvilles—The Russells—The Cecils—The Villiers—The Barings—The
Petty-Fitzmaurices—The Herberts—The Somersets—The Berkeleys—
The Seymours—The Lennoxes—The Howards.
2 vols. 8vo, £1, 8s. in extra binding, with richly-gilt cover.

BIOGRAPHICAL SKETCHES OF EMINENT SOLDIERS

OF THE LAST FOUR CENTURIES. By the late MAJOR-GENERAL
JOHN MITCHELL, Author of 'Life of Wallenstein,' the 'Fall of Napo-
leon,' &c. Edited, with a Memoir of the Author, by LEONHARD SCHMITZ,
LL.D. In Post 8vo, 9s.

ELEMENTS OF MODERN GEOGRAPHY.

For the Use of Junior Classes. By the REV. ALEX. MACKAY, A.M.,
F.R.G.S. In crown 8vo, pp. 304, 3s.

"There is no work of the kind, in the English or any other language, known to me, which comes
so near my ideal of perfection in a school-book, on the important subject of which it treats. In
arrangement, style, selection of matter, clearness, and thorough accuracy of statement, it is without
a rival; and knowing, as I do, the vast amount of labour and research bestowed on its production,
I trust it will be so appreciated as to insure, by an extensive sale, a well-merited reward."—A. Keith
Johnston, Esq., F.R.S.E., F.R.G.S., H.M. Geographer for Scotland; Author of the ' Physical Atlas,'
&c. &c.
"The best geography we have ever met with."—*Spectator.*

ADVANCED TEXT-BOOK OF PHYSICAL GEOGRAPHY.

By DAVID PAGE, F.R.S.E., F.G.S., Author of 'Introductory and
Advanced Text-Books of Geology,' &c. Crown 8vo, with a Glossary of
Terms and numerous Illustrations, 5s.

"Mr Page's volume is aptly entitled, and meets the wants of earnest and systematic students."—
Athenæum.
"A thoroughly good Text-Book of Physical Geography."—*Saturday Review.*

THE ECONOMY OF CAPITAL:

GOLD AND TRADE. By R. H. PATTERSON, Author of 'The New
Revolution,' &c. In 1 thick vol. crown 8vo, 12s. cloth.

FAMILY PRAYERS FOR TWO WEEKS.

Prepared by the Committee of the General Assembly of the Church of
Scotland on Aids to Devotion. In crown 8vo, 1s. 6d. bound in cloth, red
edges.

THE HISTORY OF SCOTLAND

From Agricola's Invasion to the Revolution of 1688. By JOHN HILL BURTON, Author of 'The Scot Abroad,' &c.

ETONIANA.

Originally published in 'Blackwood's Magazine.' 1 vol. fcap. 8vo.

THE OPERATIONS OF WAR EXPLAINED AND ILLUS-

TRATED. By COLONEL E. B. HAMLEY, R.A., late Professor of Military History, Strategy, and Tactics at the Staff College. In 1 vol. 4to, with Plans.

THE ILIAD OF HOMER.

Translated into English Verse in the Spenserian Stanza, by PHILIP STANHOPE WORSLEY, M.A., Fellow of Corpus Christi College, Oxford. Uniform with the 'Odyssey,' Translated by the Same.

ESSAYS ON SOCIAL SUBJECTS.

From the 'Saturday Review.' A Second Series, uniform with the First.

THE HANDY HORSE BOOK;

Or, Practical Instructions on Riding, Driving, and the General Care and Management of Horses. By a CAVALRY OFFICER.

DICTIONARY OF BRITISH INDIAN DATES:

Being a Compendium of all the Dates essential to the Study of the History of British Rule in India, Legal, Historical, and Biographical. Intended for Students about to face Examinations for the Indian Services.

COMPARATIVE GEOGRAPHY.

By CARL RITTER, Professor of Geography in the University of Berlin. Translated by W. L. GAGE. In crown 8vo, 3s. 6d.

DEFINITIONS IN ASTRONOMY AND NAVIGATION

MADE EASY. By the REV. J. HARBORD, M.A., R.N., Author of 'Glossary of Navigation.'

CATALOGUE

OF

MESSRS BLACKWOOD AND SONS'

PUBLICATIONS.

———◆———

HISTORY OF EUROPE,
From the Commencement of the French Revolution in 1789 to the Battle of Waterloo. By SIR ARCHIBALD ALISON, Bart., D.C.L.
A NEW LIBRARY EDITION (being the Tenth), in 14 vols. demy 8vo, with Portraits, and a copious Index, £10, 10s.
ANOTHER EDITION, in crown 8vo, 20 vols., £6.
A PEOPLE'S EDITION, 12 vols., closely printed in double columns, £2, 8s., and Index Volume, 3s.

"An extraordinary work, which has earned for itself a lasting place in the literature of the country, and within a few years found innumerable readers in every part of the globe. There is no book extant that treats so well of the period to the illustration of which Mr Alison's labours have been devoted. It exhibits great knowledge, patient research, indefatigable industry, and vast power."—*Times, Sept. 7, 1850.*

CONTINUATION OF ALISON'S HISTORY OF EUROPE,
From the Fall of Napoleon to the Accession of Louis Napoleon. By SIR ARCHIBALD ALISON, Bart., D.C.L. In 9 vols., £6, 7s. 6d. Uniform with the Library Edition of the previous work.

EPITOME OF ALISON'S HISTORY OF EUROPE.
For the Use of Schools and Young Persons. Fifteenth Edition, 7s. 6d., bound.

ATLAS TO ALISON'S HISTORY OF EUROPE;
Containing 109 Maps and Plans of Countries, Battles, Sieges, and Sea-Fights. Constructed by A. KEITH JOHNSTON, F.R.S.E. With Vocabulary of Military and Marine Terms. Demy 4to. Library Edition, £3, 3s.; People's Edition, crown 4to, £1, 11s. 6d.

LIVES OF LORD CASTLEREAGH AND SIR CHARLES STEWART, Second and Third Marquesses of Londonderry. From the Original Papers of the Family, and other sources. By SIR ARCHIBALD ALISON, Bart., D.C.L. In 3 vols. 8vo, £2, 5s.

ANNALS OF THE PENINSULAR CAMPAIGNS.
By CAPT. THOMAS HAMILTON. A New Edition. Edited by F. HARD-MAN, Esq. 8vo, 16s. ; and Atlas of Maps to illustrate the Campaigns, 12s.

A VISIT TO FLANDERS AND THE FIELD OF WATERLOO.
By JAMES SIMPSON, Advocate. A Revised Edition. With Two Coloured Plans of the Battle. Crown 8vo, 5s.

WELLINGTON'S CAREER:
A Military and Political Summary. By LIEUT.-COL. E. BRUCE HAMLEY, Professor of Military History and Art at the Staff College. Crown 8vo, 2s.

THE STORY OF THE CAMPAIGN OF SEBASTOPOL.

Written in the Camp. By LIEUT.-COL. E. BRUCE HAMLEY. With Illustrations drawn in Camp by the Author. 8vo, 21s.

"We strongly recommend this 'Story of the Campaign' to all who would gain a just comprehension of this tremendous struggle. Of this we are perfectly sure, it is a book unlikely to be ever superseded. Its truth is of that simple and startling character which is sure of an immortal existence; nor is it paying the gallant author too high a complement to class this masterpiece of military history with the most precious of those classic records which have been bequeathed to us by the great writers of antiquity who took part in the wars they have described."—*The Press.*

THE INVASION OF THE CRIMEA:

Its Origin, and Account of its Progress down to the Death of Lord Raglan. By ALEXANDER WILLIAM KINGLAKE, M.P. Vols. I. and II., bringing the Events down to the Close of the Battle of the Alma. Fourth Edition. Price 32s. To be completed in 4 vols. 8vo.

TEN YEARS OF IMPERIALISM IN FRANCE.

Impressions of a "Flâneur." Second Edition. In 8vo, price 9s.

"There has not been published for many a day a more remarkable book on France than this, which professes to be the impressions of a Flaneur. . . . It has all the liveliness and sparkle of a work written only for amusement; it has all the solidity and weight of a State paper; and we expect for it not a little political influence as a fair, full, and masterly statement of the Imperial policy—the first and only good account that has been given to Europe of the Napoleonic system now in force."—*Times.*

FLEETS AND NAVIES.

By CAPTAIN CHARLES HAMLEY, R.M. Originally published in 'Blackwood's Magazine.' Crown 8vo, 6s.

HISTORY OF GREECE UNDER FOREIGN DOMINATION.

By GEORGE FINLAY, LL.D., Athens—viz. :

GREECE UNDER THE ROMANS. B.C. 146 to A.D. 717. A Historical View of the Condition of the Greek Nation from its Conquest by the Romans until the Extinction of the Roman Power in the East. Second Edition, 16s.

HISTORY OF THE BYZANTINE EMPIRE, A.D. 716 to 1204; and of the Greek Empire of Nicæa and Constantinople, A.D. 1204 to 1453. 2 vols., £1, 7s. 6d.

MEDIEVAL GREECE AND TREBIZOND. The History of Greece, from its Conquest by the Crusaders to its Conquest by the Turks, A.D. 1204 to 1566; and the History of the Empire of Trebizond, A.D. 1204 to 1461. 12s.

GREECE UNDER OTHOMAN AND VENETIAN DOMINATION. A.D. 1453 to 1821. 10s. 6d.

HISTORY OF THE GREEK REVOLUTION. 2 vols. 8vo, £1, 4s.

"His book is worthy to take its place among the remarkable works on Greek history, which form one of the chief glories of English scholarship. The history of Greece is but half told without it."—*London Guardian.*

THE NATIONAL CHARACTER OF THE ATHENIANS.

By JOHN BROWN PATTERSON. Edited from the Author's revision, by PROFESSOR PILLANS, of the University of Edinburgh. With a Sketch of his Life. Crown 8vo, 4s. 6d.

STUDIES IN ROMAN LAW.

With Comparative Views of the Laws of France, England, and Scotland. By LORD MACKENZIE, one of the Judges of the Court of Session in Scotland. 8vo, 12s. Second Edition.

"We know not in the English language where else to look for a history of the Roman law so clear, and, at the same time, so short. . . . More improving reading, both for the general student and for the lawyer, we cannot well imagine; and there are few, even among learned professional men, who will not gather some novel information from Lord Mackenzie's simple pages."—*London Review.*

THE EIGHTEEN CHRISTIAN CENTURIES.

By the REV. JAMES WHITE. Fourth Edition, with an Analytical Table of Contents, and a Copious Index. Post 8vo, 7s. 6d.

THE MONKS OF THE WEST,

From St Benedict to St Bernard. By the COUNT DE MONTALEMBERT. Authorised Translation. 2 vols. 8vo, 21s.

HISTORY OF FRANCE,
From the Earliest Period to the Year 1848. By the Rev. JAMES WHITE, Author of 'The Eighteen Christian Centuries.' Second Edition. Post 8vo, 9s.

"An excellent and comprehensive compendium of French history, quite above the standard of a school-book, and particularly well adapted for the libraries of literary institutions."—*National Review.*

LEADERS OF THE REFORMATION:
LUTHER, CALVIN, LATIMER, and KNOX. By the Rev. JOHN TULLOCH, D.D., Principal, and Primarius Professor of Theology, St Mary's College, St Andrews. Second Edition, crown 8vo, 6s. 6d.

ENGLISH PURITANISM AND ITS LEADERS:
CROMWELL, MILTON, BAXTER, and BUNYAN. By the Rev. JOHN TULLOCH, D.D. Uniform with the 'Leaders of the Reformation.' 7s. 6d.

HISTORY OF THE FRENCH PROTESTANT REFUGEES.
By CHARLES WEISS, Professor of History at the Lycée Buonaparte. Translated by F. HARDMAN, Esq. 8vo, 14s.

HISTORY OF THE CHURCH OF SCOTLAND,
From the Reformation to the Revolution Settlement. By the Very Rev. JOHN LEE, D.D., LL.D., Principal of the University of Edinburgh. Edited by the Rev. WILLIAM LEE. 2 vols. 8vo, 21s.

HISTORY OF SCOTLAND FROM THE REVOLUTION
To the Extinction of the last Jacobite Insurrection, 1689-1748. By JOHN HILL BURTON, Esq., Advocate. 2 vols. 8vo, reduced to 15s.

LIVES OF THE QUEENS OF SCOTLAND,
And English Princesses connected with the Regal Succession of Great Britain. By AGNES STRICKLAND. With Portraits and Historical Vignettes. Post 8vo, £4, 4s.

"Every step in Scotland is historical: the shades of the dead arise on every side; the very rocks breathe. Miss Strickland's talents as a writer, and turn of mind as an individual, in a peculiar manner fit her for painting a historical gallery of the most illustrious or dignified female characters in that land of chivalry and song."—*Blackwood's Magazine.*

MEMORIALS OF THE CASTLE OF EDINBURGH.
By JAMES GRANT, Esq. A New Edition. In crown 8vo, with 12 Engravings, 3s. 6d.

MEMOIRS OF SIR WILLIAM KIRKALDY OF GRANGE,
Governor of the Castle of Edinburgh for Mary Queen of Scots. By JAMES GRANT, Esq. Post 8vo, 10s. 6d.

MEMOIRS OF SIR JOHN HEPBURN,
Marshal of France under Louis XIII., &c. By JAMES GRANT, Esq. Post 8vo, 8s.

WORKS OF THE REV. THOMAS M'CRIE, D.D.
A New and Uniform Edition. Edited by Professor M'CRIE. 4 vols. crown 8vo, 24s. Sold separately—viz.:

LIFE OF JOHN KNOX. Containing Illustrations of the History of the Reformation in Scotland. Crown 8vo, 6s.

LIFE OF ANDREW MELVILLE. Containing Illustrations of the Ecclesiastical and Literary History of Scotland in the Sixteenth and Seventeenth Centuries. Crown 8vo, 6s.

HISTORY OF THE PROGRESS AND SUPPRESSION OF THE REFORMATION IN ITALY IN THE SIXTEENTH CENTURY. Crown 8vo, 4s.

HISTORY OF THE PROGRESS AND SUPPRESSION OF THE REFORMATION IN SPAIN IN THE SIXTEENTH CENTURY. Crown 8vo, 3s. 6d.

THE BOSCOBEL TRACTS;

Relating to the Escape of Charles the Second after the Battle of Worcester, and his subsequent Adventures. Edited by J. HUGHES, Esq., A.M. A New Edition, with additional Notes and Illustrations, including Communications from the Rev. R. H. BARHAM, Author of the 'Ingoldsby Legends.' In 8vo, with Engravings, 16s.

"'The Boscobel Tracts' is a very curious book, and about as good an example of single subject historical collections as may be found. Originally undertaken, or at least completed, at the suggestion of the late Bishop Copplestone, in 1827, it was carried out with a degree of judgment and taste not always found in works of a similar character."—*Spectator.*

LIFE OF JOHN DUKE OF MARLBOROUGH.

With some Account of his Contemporaries, and of the War of the Succession. By SIR ARCHIBALD ALISON, Bart., D.C.L. Third Edition. 2 vols. 8vo, Portraits and Maps, 30s.

THE NEW 'EXAMEN;'

Or, An Inquiry into the Evidence of certain Passages in 'Macaulay's History of England' concerning—THE DUKE OF MARLBOROUGH—THE MASSACRE OF GLENCOE—THE HIGHLANDS OF SCOTLAND—VISCOUNT DUNDEE—WILLIAM PENN. By JOHN PAGET, Esq., Barrister-at-Law. In crown 8vo, 6s.

"We certainly never saw a more damaging exposure, and it is something worth notice that much of it appeared in 'Blackwood's Magazine' during the lifetime of Lord Macaulay, but he never attempted to make any reply. The charges are so direct, and urged in such unmistakable language, that no writer who valued his character for either accuracy of fact or fairness in comment would let them remain unanswered if he had any reason to give."—*Gentleman's Magazine.*

AUTOBIOGRAPHY OF THE REV. DR CARLYLE,

Minister of Inveresk. Containing Memorials of the Men and Events of his Time. Edited by JOHN HILL BURTON. In 8vo. Third Edition, with Portrait, 14s.

"This book contains by far the most vivid picture of Scottish life and manners that has been given to the public since the days of Sir Walter Scott. In bestowing upon it this high praise, we make no exception, not even in favour of Lord Cockburn's 'Memorials'—the book which resembles it most, and which ranks next to it in interest."—*Edinburgh Review.*

MEMOIR OF THE POLITICAL LIFE OF EDMUND BURKE.

With Extracts from his Writings. By the REV. GEORGE CROLY, D.D. 2 vols. post 8vo, 18s.

CURRAN AND HIS CONTEMPORARIES.

By CHARLES PHILLIPS, Esq., A.B. A New Edition. Crown 8vo, 7s. 6d.

"Certainly one of the most extraordinary pieces of biography ever produced. . . . . . No library should be without it."—*Lord Brougham.*
"Never, perhaps, was there a more curious collection of portraits crowded before into the same canvas."—*Times.*

MEMOIR OF MRS HEMANS.

By her SISTER. With a Portrait. Fcap. 8vo, 5s.

LIFE OF THE LATE REV. JAMES ROBERTSON, D.D.,

F.R.S.E., Professor of Divinity and Ecclesiastical History in the University of Edinburgh. By the Rev. A. H. CHARTERIS, M.A., Minister of Newabbey. With a Portrait. 8vo, price 10s. 6d.

ESSAYS; HISTORICAL, POLITICAL, AND MISCELLANEOUS.

By SIR ARCHIBALD ALISON, Bart. 3 vols. demy 8vo, 45s.

ESSAYS IN HISTORY AND ART.

By R. H. PATTERSON. Viz.:

COLOUR IN NATURE AND ART—REAL AND IDEAL BEAUTY—SCULPTURE—ETHNOLOGY OF EUROPE—UTOPIAS—OUR INDIAN EMPIRE—THE NATIONAL LIFE OF CHINA—AN IDEAL ART-CONGRESS—BATTLE OF THE STYLES—GENIUS AND LIBERTY—YOUTH AND SUMMER—RECORDS OF THE PAST: NINEVEH AND BABYLON—INDIA: ITS CASTES AND CREEDS—"CHRISTOPHER NORTH:" IN MEMORIAM. In 1 vol. 8vo, 12s.

NORMAN SINCLAIR.
By W. E. AYTOUN, D.C.L., Author of 'Lays of the Scottish Cavaliers,' &c. &c. In 3 vols. post 8vo, 31s. 6d.

THE OLD BACHELOR IN THE OLD SCOTTISH VILLAGE.
By THOMAS AIRD. Fcap. 8vo, 4s.

SIR EDWARD BULWER LYTTON'S NOVELS.
Library Edition. Printed from a large and readable type. In Volumes of a convenient and handsome form. 8vo, 5s. each—viz.:

THE CAXTON NOVELS, 10 Volumes:

The Caxton Family. 2 vols.	What will he do with it?
My Novel. 4 vols.	4 vols.

HISTORICAL ROMANCES, 11 Volumes:

Devereux. 2 vols.	The Siege of Grenada. 1 vol.
The Last Days of Pompeii. 2 vols.	The Last of the Barons. 2 vols.
Rienzi. 2 vols.	Harold. 2 vols.

ROMANCES, 5 Volumes:

The Pilgrims of the Rhine.	Eugene Aram. 2 vols.
1 vol.	Zanoni. 2 vols.

NOVELS OF LIFE AND MANNERS, 15 Volumes:

Pelham. 2 vols.	Ernest Maltravers — Second Part (i.e. Alice.)
The Disowned. 2 vols.	2 vols.
Paul Clifford. 2 vols.	Night and Morning.
Godolphin. 1 vol.	2 vols.
Ernest Maltravers—First Part.	Lucretia. 2 vols.
2 vols.	

"It is of the handiest of sizes; the paper is good; and the type, which seems to be new, is very clear and beautiful. There are no pictures. The whole charm of the presentment of the volume consists in its handiness, and the tempting clearness and beauty of the type, which almost converts into a pleasure the mere act of following the printer's lines, and leaves the author's mind free to exert its unobstructed force upon the reader."—*Examiner.*
" Nothing could be better as to size, type, paper, and general get-up."—*Athenæum.*

JESSIE CAMERON: A HIGHLAND STORY.
By the LADY RACHEL BUTLER. Second Edition. Small 8vo, with a Frontispiece, 2s. 6d.

SOME PASSAGES IN THE LIFE OF ADAM BLAIR,
And History of Matthew Wald. By the Author of 'Valerius.' Fcap. 8vo, 4s. cloth.

CAPTAIN CLUTTERBUCK'S CHAMPAGNE:
A West Indian Reminiscence. Post 8vo, 12s.

SCENES OF CLERICAL LIFE.
The Sad Fortunes of Amos Barton—Mr Gilfil's Love-Story—Janet's Repentance. By GEORGE ELIOT. 2 vols. fcap. 8vo, 12s.

ADAM BEDE.
By GEORGE ELIOT. 2 vols. fcap. 8vo, 12s.

THE MILL ON THE FLOSS.
By GEORGE ELIOT. 2 vols. fcap. 8vo, 12s.

SILAS MARNER: THE WEAVER OF RAVELOE.
By GEORGE ELIOT. Fcap. 8vo, 6s.

THE NOVELS OF GEORGE ELIOT.
Cheap Edition, complete in 3 vols., price 6s. each—viz.:
ADAM BEDE.
THE MILL ON THE FLOSS.
SCENES OF CLERICAL LIFE, and SILAS MARNER.

ANNALS OF THE PARISH, AND AYRSHIRE LEGATEES.
By JOHN GALT.   Fcap. 8vo, 4s. cloth.

SIR ANDREW WYLIE.
By JOHN GALT.   Fcap. 8vo, 4s. cloth.

THE PROVOST, AND OTHER TALES.
By JOHN GALT.   Fcap. 8vo, 4s. cloth.

THE ENTAIL.
By JOHN GALT.   Fcap. 8vo, 4s. cloth.

THE YOUTH AND MANHOOD OF CYRIL THORNTON.
By CAPTAIN HAMILTON.   Fcap. 8vo, 4s. cloth.

LADY LEE'S WIDOWHOOD.
By LIEUT.-COL. E. B. HAMLEY.   Crown 8vo, with 13 Illustrations by the
Author.   6s.

THE LIFE OF MANSIE WAUCH,
Tailor in Dalkeith.   By D. M. MOIR.   Fcap. 8vo, 3s. cloth.

NIGHTS AT MESS, SIR FRIZZLE PUMPKIN, AND OTHER
TALES.   Fcap. 8vo, 3s. cloth.

KATIE STEWART: A TRUE STORY.
By MRS OLIPHANT.   Fcap. 8vo, with Frontispiece and Vignette.   4s.

PEN OWEN.
Fcap. 8vo, 4s. cloth.

PENINSULAR SCENES AND SKETCHES.
Fcap. 8vo, 3s. cloth.

REGINALD DALTON.
By the Author of 'Valerius.'   Fcap. 8vo, 4s. cloth.

LIFE IN THE FAR WEST.
By G. F. RUXTON, Esq.   Second Edition.   Fcap. 8vo, 4s.

TOM CRINGLE'S LOG.
A New Edition.   With Illustrations by STANFIELD, WEIR, SKELTON, WALKER,
&c., Engraved by WHYMPER.   Crown 8vo, 6s.
"Everybody who has failed to read 'Tom Cringle's Log' should do so at once. The 'Quarterly Review' went so far as to say that the papers composing it, when it first appeared in 'Blackwood,' were
the most brilliant series of the time, and that time one unrivalled for the number of famous magazinists
existing in it. Coleridge says, in his 'Table Talk,' that the 'Log' is most excellent; and these verdicts
have been ratified by generations of men and boys, and by the manifestation of Continental approval
which is shown by repeated translations. The engravings illustrating the present issue are excellent."—
Standard.

TOM CRINGLE'S LOG.
Fcap. 8vo, 4s. cloth.

THE CRUISE OF THE MIDGE.
By the Author of 'Tom Cringle's Log.'   Fcap. 8vo, 4s. cloth.

CHAPTERS ON CHURCHYARDS.
By MRS SOUTHEY.   Fcap. 8vo, 7s. 6d.

THE SUBALTERN.
By the Author of the 'The Chelsea Pensioners.'   Fcap. 8vo, 3s. cloth.

CHRONICLES OF CARLINGFORD: SALEM CHAPEL.
Second Edition. Complete in 1 vol., price 5s.

"This story, so fresh, so powerfully written, and so tragic, stands out from among its fellows like a piece of newly-coined gold in a handful of dim commonplace shillings. Tales of pastoral experience and scenes from clerical life we have had in plenty, but the sacred things of the conventicle, the relative position of pastor and flock in a Nonconforming 'connection,' were but guessed at by the world outside, and terrible is the revelation."—*Westminster Review.*

CHRONICLES OF CARLINGFORD: THE RECTOR, AND THE DOCTOR'S FAMILY. Post 8vo, 12s.

TALES FROM BLACKWOOD.
Complete in 12 vols., bound in cloth, 18s. The Volumes are sold separately, 1s. 6d. ; and may be had of most Booksellers, in Six Volumes, handsomely half-bound in red morocco.

CONTENTS.

VOL. I. The Glenmutchkin Railway.—Vanderdecken's Message Home.—The Floating Beacon.—Colonna the Painter.—Napoleon.—A Legend of Gibraltar.—The Iron Shroud.

VOL. II. Lazaro's Legacy.—A Story without a Tail.—Faustus and Queen Elizabeth.—How I became a Yeoman.—Devereux Hall.—The Metempsychosis.—College Theatricals.

VOL. III. A Reading Party in the Long Vacation.—Father Tom and the Pope.—La Petite Madelaine. — Bob Burke's Duel with Ensign Brady. — The Headsman : A Tale of Doom.—The Wearyful Woman.

VOL. IV. How I stood for the Dreepdaily Burghs.—First and Last.—The Duke's Dilemma : A Chronicle of Niesenstein.—The Old Gentleman's Teetotum.—"Woe to us when we lose the Watery Wall."—My College Friends : Charles Russell, the Gentleman Commoner.—The Magic Lay of the One-Horse Chay.

VOL. V. Adventures in Texas.—How we got Possession of the Tuileries.—Captain Paton's Lament.—The Village Doctor.—A Singular Letter from Southern Africa.

VOL. VI. My Friend the Dutchman.—My College Friends—No. II.: Horace Leicester.—The Emerald Studs.—My College Friends—No. III.: Mr W. Wellington Hurst.—Christine : A Dutch Story.—The Man in the Bell.

VOL. VII. My English Acquaintance.—The Murderer's Last Night.—Narration of Certain Uncommon Things that did formerly happen to Me, Herbert Willis, B.D.—The Wags.—The Wet Wooing : A Narrative of '98.—Ben-na-Groich.

VOL. VIII. The Surveyor's Tale. By Professor Aytoun.—The Forrest Race Romance.—Di Vasari : A Tale of Florence. —Sigismund Fatello. — The Boxes.

VOL. IX. Rosaura : A Tale of Madrid.—Adventure in the North-West Territory.—Harry Bolton's Curacy.—The Florida Pirate.—The Pandour and his Princess.—The Beauty Draught.

VOL. X. Antonio di Carara.—The Fatal Repast.—The Vision of Cagliostro.—The First and Last Kiss.—The Smuggler's Leap.—The Haunted and the Haunters.—The Duellists.

VOL. XI. The Natolian Story-Teller.—The First and Last Crime.—John Rintoul.—Major Moss.—The Premier and his Wife.

VOL. XII. Tickler among the Thieves !—The Bridegroom of Barna.—The Involuntary Experimentalist.—Lebrun's Lawsuit.—The Snowing-up of Strath Lugas.—A Few Words on Social Philosophy.

THE WONDER-SEEKER;
Or, The History of Charles Douglas. By M. FRASER TYTLER, Author of 'Tales of the Great and Brave,' &c. A New Edition. Fcap. 8vo, 3s. 6d.

VALERIUS: A ROMAN STORY.
Fcap. 8vo, 3s. cloth.

THE DIARY OF A LATE PHYSICIAN.
By SAMUEL WARREN, D.C.L. 1 vol. crown 8vo, 5s. 6d.

TEN THOUSAND A-YEAR.
By SAMUEL WARREN, D.C.L. 2 vols. crown 8vo, 9s.

NOW AND THEN.
By SAMUEL WARREN, D.C.L. Crown 8vo, 2s. 6d.

THE LILY AND THE BEE.
By SAMUEL WARREN, D.C.L. Crown 8vo, 2s.

MISCELLANIES.
By SAMUEL WARREN, D.C.L. Crown 8vo, 5s.

WORKS OF SAMUEL WARREN, D.C.L.
Uniform Edition. 5 vols. crown 8vo, 24s.

WORKS OF PROFESSOR WILSON.
Edited by his Son-in-Law, Professor FERRIER. In 12 vols. crown 8vo, £3, 12s.

RECREATIONS OF CHRISTOPHER NORTH.
By PROFESSOR WILSON. In 2 vols. crown 8vo, 12s.

THE NOCTES AMBROSIANÆ.
By PROFESSOR WILSON. With Notes and a Glossary. In 4 vols. crown 8vo, 24s.

A CHEAP EDITION OF THE NOCTES AMBROSIANÆ.
In 12 Parts, price 1s. each, forming Four Volumes at 4s. each in cloth.

LIGHTS AND SHADOWS OF SCOTTISH LIFE.
By PROFESSOR WILSON. Fcap. 8vo, 3s. cloth.

THE TRIALS OF MARGARET LYNDSAY.
By PROFESSOR WILSON. Fcap. 8vo, 3s. cloth.

THE FORESTERS.
By PROFESSOR WILSON. Fcap. 8vo, 3s. cloth.

TALES.
By PROFESSOR WILSON. Comprising 'The Lights and Shadows of Scottish Life;' 'The Trials of Margaret Lyndsay;' and 'The Foresters.' In 1 vol. crown 8vo, 6s. cloth.

ESSAYS, CRITICAL AND IMAGINATIVE.
By PROFESSOR WILSON. 4 vols. crown 8vo, 24s.

THE BOOK-HUNTER, ETC.
By JOHN HILL BURTON. New Edition. In crown 8vo, 7s. 6d.

" A book pleasant to look at and pleasant to read—pleasant from its rich store of anecdote, its geniality, and its humour, even to persons who care little for the subjects of which it treats, but beyond measure delightful to those who are in any degree members of the above-mentioned fraternity."—*Saturday Review.*

" We have not been more amused for a long time : and every reader who takes interest in typography and its consequences will say the same, if he will begin to read ; beginning, he will finish, and be sorry when it is over."—*Athenæum.*

" Mr Burton has now given us a pleasant book, full of quaint anecdote, and of a lively bookish talk. There is a quiet humour in it which is very taking, and there is a curious knowledge of books which is really very sound."—*Examiner.*

HOMER AND HIS TRANSLATORS,
And the Greek Drama. By PROFESSOR WILSON. Crown 8vo, 6s.

" But of all the criticisms on Homer which I have ever had the good fortune to read, in our own or any language, the most vivid and entirely genial are those found in the ' Essays, Critical and Imaginative,' of the late Professor Wilson."—*Mr Gladstone's Studies on Homer.*

THE SKETCHER.
By the REV. JOHN EAGLES. Originally published in 'Blackwood's Magazine.' 8vo, 10s. 6d.

" This volume, called by the appropriate name of ' The Sketcher,' is one that ought to be found in the studio of every English landscape-painter. . . . . More instructive and suggestive readings for young artists, especially landscape-painters, can scarcely be found."—*The Globe.*

ESSAYS.
By the REV. JOHN EAGLES, A.M. Oxon. Originally published in 'Blackwood's Magazine.' Post 8vo, 10s. 6d.

CONTENTS :—Church Music, and other Parochials.—Medical Attendance, and other Parochials.—A few Hours at Hampton Court.—Grandfathers and Grandchildren.—Sitting for a Portrait.—Are there not Great Boasters among us?—Temperance and Teetotal Societies.—Thackeray's Lectures : Swift. —The Crystal Palace. —Civilisation : The Census. —The Beggar's Legacy.

ESSAYS; HISTORICAL, POLITICAL, AND MISCELLANEOUS.
By SIR ARCHIBALD ALISON, Bart., D.C.L. Three vols., demy 8vo, 45s.

LECTURES ON THE POETICAL LITERATURE OF THE
PAST HALF-CENTURY. By D. M. MOIR. Third Edition. Fcap. 8vo, 5s.

" Exquisite in its taste and generous in its criticisms."—*Hugh Miller.*

LECTURES ON THE HISTORY OF LITERATURE,
Ancient and Modern. From the German of F. SCHLEGEL. Fcap., 5s.

" A wonderful performance—better than anything we as yet have in our own language."—*Quarterly Review.*

THE GENIUS OF HANDEL,
And the distinctive Character of his Sacred Compositions. Two Lectures. Delivered to the Members of the Edinburgh Philosophical Institution. By the VERY REV. DEAN RAMSAY, Author of ' Reminiscences of Scottish Life and Character.' In crown 8vo, 3s. 6d.

BLACKWOOD'S MAGAZINE,
From Commencement in 1817 to December 1861. Numbers 1 to 554, forming 90 Volumes. £31, 10s.

INDEX TO THE FIRST FIFTY VOLUMES OF BLACKWOOD'S
MAGAZINE. 8vo, 15s.

LAYS OF THE SCOTTISH CAVALIERS,

And other Poems. By W. EDMONDSTOUNE AYTOUN, D.C.L., Professor of Rhetoric and English Literature in the University of Edinburgh. Fourteenth Edition. Fcap. 8vo, 7s. 6d.

"Professor Aytoun's 'Lays of the Scottish Cavaliers'—a volume of verse which shows that Scotland has yet a poet. Full of the true fire, it now stirs and swells like a trumpet-note—now sinks in cadences sad and wild as the wail of a Highland dirge."—*Quarterly Review.*

BOTHWELL : A POEM.

By W. EDMONDSTOUNE AYTOUN, D.C.L. Third Edition. Fcap. 8vo, 7s. 6d.

"Professor Aytoun has produced a fine poem and an able argument, and 'Bothwell' will assuredly take its stand among the classics of Scottish literature."—*The Press.*

THE BALLADS OF SCOTLAND.

Edited by Professor AYTOUN. Second Edition. 2 vols. fcap. 8vo, 12s.

"No country can boast of a richer collection of Ballads than Scotland, and no Editor for these Ballads could be found more accomplished than Professor Aytoun. He has sent forth two beautiful volumes which range with 'Percy's Reliques'—which, for completeness and accuracy, leave little to be desired—which must henceforth be considered as the standard edition of the Scottish Ballads, and which we commend as a model to any among ourselves who may think of doing like service to the English Ballads."—*Times.*

POEMS AND BALLADS OF GOETHE.

Translated by Professor AYTOUN and THEODORE MARTIN. Second Edition. Fcap. 8vo, 6s.

"There is no doubt that these are the best translations of Goethe's marvellously-cut gems which have yet been published."—*Times.*

THE BOOK OF BALLADS.

Edited by BON GAULTIER. Seventh Edition, with numerous Illustrations by DOYLE, LEECH, and CROWQUILL. Gilt edges, post 8vo, 8s. 6d.

FIRMILIAN; OR, THE STUDENT OF BADAJOS.

A Spasmodic Tragedy. By T. PERCY JONES. In small 8vo, 5s.

"Humour of a kind most rare at all times, and especially in the present day, runs through every page, and passages of true poetry and delicious versification prevent the continual play of sarcasm from becoming tedious."—*Literary Gazette.*

POETICAL WORKS OF THOMAS AIRD.

Fourth Edition. In 1 vol. fcap. 8vo, 6s.

POEMS.

By the LADY FLORA HASTINGS. Edited by her SISTER. Second Edition, with a Portrait. Fcap., 7s. 6d.

THE POEMS OF FELICIA HEMANS.

Complete in 1 vol. royal 8vo, with Portrait by FINDEN. Cheap Edition, 12s. 6d. *Another Edition*, with MEMOIR by her SISTER. Seven vols. fcap., 35s. *Another Edition*, in 6 vols., cloth, gilt edges, 24s.

The following Works of Mrs HEMANS are sold separately, bound in cloth, gilt edges, 4s. each :—

RECORDS OF WOMAN. FOREST SANCTUARY. SONGS OF THE AFFECTIONS. DRAMATIC WORKS. TALES AND HISTORIC SCENES. MORAL AND RELIGIOUS POEMS.

THE ODYSSEY OF HOMER.

Translated into English Verse in the Spenserian Stanza. By PHILIP STANHOPE WORSLEY, M.A., Scholar of Corpus Christi College. 2 vols. crown 8vo, 18s.

"Mr Worsley,—applying the Spenserian stanza, that beautiful romantic measure, to the most romantic poem of the ancient world—making the stanza yield him, too (what it never yielded to Byron), its treasures of fluidity and sweet ease—above all, bringing to his task a truly poetical sense and skill,—has produced a version of the 'Odyssey' much the most pleasing of those hitherto produced, and which is delightful to read."—*Professor Arnold on Translating Homer.*

POEMS AND TRANSLATIONS.
By PHILIP STANHOPE WORSLEY, M.A., Scholar of Corpus Christi College, Oxford. Fcap. 8vo, 5s.

POEMS.
By ISA. In small 8vo, 4s. 6d.

POETICAL WORKS OF D. M. MOIR. .
With Portrait, and Memoir by THOMAS AIRD. Second Edition. 2 vols. fcap. 8vo, 12s.

LECTURES ON THE POETICAL LITERATURE OF THE PAST HALF-CENTURY. By D. M. MOIR (Δ). Second Edition. Fcap. 8vo, 5s.
" A delightful volume."—*Morning Chronicle.*
" Exquisite in its taste and generous in its criticisms."—*Hugh Miller.*

THE COURSE OF TIME: A POEM.
By ROBERT POLLOK, A.M. Twenty-third Edition. Fcap. 8vo, 5s.
" Of deep and hallowed impress, full of noble thoughts and graphic conceptions—the production of a mind alive to the great relations of being, and the sublime simplicity of our religion."—*Blackwood's Magazine.*

AN ILLUSTRATED EDITION OF THE COURSE OF TIME.
In large 8vo, bound in cloth, richly gilt, 21s.
" There has been no modern poem in the English language, of the class to which the 'Course of Time' belongs, since Milton wrote, that can be compared to it. In the present instance the artistic talents of Messrs FOSTER, CLAYTON, TENNIEL, EVANS, DALZIEL, GREEN, and WOODS, have been employed in giving expression to the sublimity of the language, by equally exquisite illustrations, all of which are of the highest class."—*Bell's Messenger.*

POEMS AND BALLADS OF SCHILLER.
Translated by Sir EDWARD BULWER LYTTON, Bart. Second Edition. 8vo, 10s. 6d.

ST STEPHEN'S;
Or, Illustrations of Parliamentary Oratory. A Poem. *Comprising*—Pym—Vane—Strafford—Halifax—Shaftesbury—St John—Sir R. Walpole—Chesterfield—Carteret—Chatham—Pitt—Fox—Burke—Sheridan—Wilberforce—Wyndham—Conway—Castlereagh—William Lamb (Lord Melbourne)—Tierney—Lord Grey—O'Connell—Plunkett—Shiel—Follett—Macaulay—Peel. Second Edition. Crown 8vo, 5s.

LEGENDS, LYRICS, AND OTHER POEMS.
By B. SIMMONS. Fcap., 7s. 6d.

SIR WILLIAM CRICHTON—ATHELWOLD—GUIDONE:
Dramas by WILLIAM SMITH, Author of 'Thorndale,' &c. 32mo, 2s. 6d.

THE BIRTHDAY, AND OTHER POEMS.
By MRS SOUTHEY. Second Edition, 5s.

ILLUSTRATIONS OF THE LYRIC POETRY AND MUSIC OF SCOTLAND. By WILLIAM STENHOUSE. Originally compiled to accompany the 'Scots Musical Museum,' and now published separately, with Additional Notes and Illustrations. 8vo, 7s. 6d.

PROFESSOR WILSON'S POEMS.
Containing the 'Isle of Palms,' the 'City of the Plague,' 'Unimore,' and other Poems. Complete Edition. Crown 8vo, 6s.

POEMS AND SONGS.
By DAVID WINGATE. Second Edition. Fcap. 8vo, 5s.
" We are delighted to welcome into the brotherhood of real poets a countryman of Burns, and whose verse will go far to render the rougher Border Scottish a classic dialect in our literature."—*John Bull.*

THE PHYSICAL ATLAS OF NATURAL PHENOMENA.

By ALEXANDER KEITH JOHNSTON, F.R.S.E., &c., Geographer to the Queen for Scotland. A New and Enlarged Edition, consisting of 35 Folio Plates, and 27 smaller ones, printed in Colours, with 135 pages of Letterpress, and Index. Imperial folio, half-bound morocco, £8, 8s.

"A perfect treasure of compressed information."—*Sir John Herschel.*

THE PHYSICAL ATLAS.

By ALEXANDER KEITH JOHNSTON, F.R.S.E., &c. Reduced from the Imperial Folio. This Edition contains Twenty-five Maps, including a Palæontological and Geological Map of the British Islands, with Descriptive Letterpress, and a very copious Index. In imperial 4to, half-bound morocco, £2, 12s. 6d.

"Executed with remarkable care, and is as accurate, and, for all educational purposes, as valuable, as the splendid large work (by the same author) which has now a European reputation."—*Eclectic Review.*

A GEOLOGICAL MAP OF EUROPE.

By SIR R. I. MURCHISON, D.C.L., F.R.S., &c., Director-General of the Geological Survey of Great Britain and Ireland; and JAMES NICOL, F.R.S.E., F.G.S., Professor of Natural History in the University of Aberdeen. Constructed by ALEXANDER KEITH JOHNSTON, F.R.S.E., &c. Four Sheets imperial, beautifully printed in Colours. In Sheets, £3, 3s.; in a Cloth Case, 4to, £3, 10s.

GEOLOGICAL AND PALÆONTOLOGICAL MAP OF THE

BRITISH ISLANDS, including Tables of the Fossils of the different Epochs, &c. &c., from the Sketches and Notes of Professor EDWARD FORBES. With Illustrative and Explanatory Letterpress. 21s.

GEOLOGICAL MAP OF SCOTLAND.

By JAMES NICOL, F.R.S.E., &c., Professor of Natural History in the University of Aberdeen. With Explanatory Notes. The Topography by ALEXANDER KEITH JOHNSTON, F.R.S.E., &c. Scale, 10 miles to an inch. In Cloth Case, 21s.

INTRODUCTORY TEXT-BOOK OF PHYSICAL GEOGRAPHY.

By DAVID PAGE, F.R.S.E., &c. With Illustrations and a Glossarial Index. Crown 8vo, 2s.

INTRODUCTORY TEXT-BOOK OF GEOLOGY.

By DAVID PAGE, F.R.S.E., F.G.S. With Engravings on Wood and Glossarial Index. Fifth Edition, 1s. 9d.

"It has not often been our good fortune to examine a text-book on science of which we could express an opinion so entirely favourable as we are enabled to do of Mr Page's little work."—*Athenæum.*

ADVANCED TEXT-BOOK OF GEOLOGY,

Descriptive and Industrial. By DAVID PAGE, F.R.S.E., F.G.S. With Engravings and Glossary of Scientific Terms. Third Edition, revised and enlarged, 6s.

"It is therefore with unfeigned pleasure that we record our appreciation of his 'Advanced Text-Book of Geology.' We have carefully read this truly satisfactory book, and do not hesitate to say that it is an excellent compendium of the great facts of Geology, and written in a truthful and philosophic spirit."—*Edinburgh Philosophical Journal.*

HANDBOOK OF GEOLOGICAL TERMS AND GEOLOGY.

By DAVID PAGE, F.R.S.E., F.G.S. In crown 8vo, 6s.

THE PAST AND PRESENT LIFE OF THE GLOBE:

Being a Sketch in Outline of the World's Life-System. By DAVID PAGE, F.R.S.E., F.G.S. Crown 8vo, 6s. With Fifty Illustrations, drawn and engraved expressly for this Work.

"Mr Page, whose admirable text-books of geology have already secured him a position of importance in the scientific world, will add considerably to his reputation by the present sketch, as he modestly terms it, of the Life-System, or gradual evolution of the vitality of our globe. In no manual that we are aware of have the facts and phenomena of biology been presented in at once so systematic and succinct a form, the successive manifestations of life on the earth set forth in so clear an order, or traced so vividly from the earliest organisms deep-buried in its stratified crust, to the familiar forms that now adorn and people its surface."—*Literary Gazette.*

THE GEOLOGICAL EXAMINATOR:
A Progressive Series of Questions adapted to the Introductory and Advanced Text-Books of Geology. Prepared to assist Teachers in framing their Examinations, and Students in testing their own Progress and Proficiency. By DAVID PAGE, F.R.S.E., F.G.S. Second Edition, 6d.

THE GEOLOGY OF PENNSYLVANIA:
A Government Survey; with a General View of the Geology of the United States, Essays on the Coal-Formation and its Fossils, and a Description of the Coal-Fields of North America and Great Britain. By PROFESSOR HENRY DARWIN ROGERS, F.R.S., F.G.S., Professor of Natural History in the University of Glasgow. With Seven large Maps, and numerous Illustrations engraved on Copper and on Wood. In 3 vols. royal 4to, £8, 8s.

SEA-SIDE STUDIES AT ILFRACOMBE, TENBY, THE SCILLY ISLES, AND JERSEY. By GEORGE HENRY LEWES. Second Edition. Crown 8vo, with Illustrations, and a Glossary of Technical Terms, 6s. 6d.

PHYSIOLOGY OF COMMON LIFE.
By GEORGE HENRY LEWES, Author of 'Sea-side Studies,' &c. Illustrated with numerous Engravings. 2 vols., 12s.

CHEMISTRY OF COMMON LIFE.
By PROFESSOR J. F. W. JOHNSTON. A New Edition. Edited by G. H. LEWES. With 113 Illustrations on Wood, and a Copious Index. 2 vols. crown 8vo, 11s. 6d.

NOMENCLATURE OF COLOURS,
Applicable to the Arts and Natural Sciences, to Manufactures, and other Purposes of General Utility. By D. R. HAY, F.R.S.E. 228 Examples of Colours, Hues, Tints, and Shades. 8vo, £3, 3s.

NARRATIVE OF THE EARL OF ELGIN'S MISSION TO CHINA AND JAPAN. By LAURENCE OLIPHANT, Private Secretary to Lord Elgin. Illustrated with numerous Engravings in Chromo-Lithography, Maps, and Engravings on Wood, from Original Drawings and Photographs. Second Edition. In 2 vols. 8vo, 21s.

"The volumes in which Mr Oliphant has related these transactions will be read with the strongest interest now, and deserve to retain a permanent place in the literary and historical annals of our time."—*Edinburgh Review.*

RUSSIAN SHORES OF THE BLACK SEA
In the Autumn of 1852. With a Voyage down the Volga and a Tour through the Country of the Don Cossacks. By LAURENCE OLIPHANT, Esq. 8vo, with Map and other Illustrations. Fourth Edition, 14s.

EGYPT, THE SOUDAN, AND CENTRAL AFRICA:
With Explorations from Khartoum on the White Nile to the Regions of the Equator. By JOHN PETHERICK, F.R.G.S., Her Britannic Majesty's Consul for the Soudan. In 8vo, with a Map, 16s.

NOTES ON NORTH AMERICA:
Agricultural, Economical, and Social. By PROFESSOR J. F. W. JOHNSTON. 2 vols. post 8vo, 21s.

"Professor Johnston's admirable Notes . . . . The very best manual for intelligent emigrants, whilst to the British agriculturist and general reader it conveys a more complete conception of the condition of these prosperous regions than all that has hitherto been written."—*Economist.*

A FAMILY TOUR ROUND THE COASTS OF SPAIN AND PORTUGAL during the Winter of 1860-1861. By LADY DUNBAR, of Northfield. In post 8vo, 5s.

THE ROYAL ATLAS OF MODERN GEOGRAPHY.

In a Series of entirely Original and Authentic Maps. By A. KEITH JOHNSTON, F.R.S.E., F.R.G.S., Author of the ' Physical Atlas,' &c. With a complete Index of easy reference to each Map, comprising nearly 150,000 Places contained in this Atlas. Imperial folio, half-bound in russia or morocco, £5, 15s. 6d. (Dedicated by permission to Her Majesty.)

" No one can look through Mr Keith Johnston's new Atlas without seeing that it is the best which has ever been published in this country."—The Times.

" Of the many noble atlases prepared by Mr Johnston and published by Messrs Blackwood & Sons, this Royal Atlas will be the most useful to the public, and will deserve to be the most popular."—Athenæum.

" We know no series of maps which we can more warmly recommend. The accuracy, wherever we have attempted to put it to the test, is really astonishing."—Saturday Review.

" The culmination of all attempts to depict the face of the world appears in the Royal Atlas, than which it is impossible to conceive anything more perfect."—Morning Herald.

" This is, beyond question, the most splendid and luxurious, as well as the most useful and complete, of all existing atlases."—Guardian.

" There has not, we believe, been produced for general public use a body of maps equal in beauty and completeness to the Royal Atlas just issued by Mr A. K. Johnston."—Examiner.

" An almost daily reference to, and comparison of it with others, since the publication of the first part some two years ago until now, enables us to say, without the slightest hesitation, that this is by far the most complete and authentic atlas that has yet been issued."—Scotsman.

" Beyond doubt the greatest geographical work of our time."—Museum.

INDEX GEOGRAPHICUS:

Being an Index to nearly ONE HUNDRED AND FIFTY THOUSAND NAMES OF PLACES, &c.; with their LATITUDES and LONGITUDES as given in KEITH JOHNSTON'S ' ROYAL ATLAS ;' together with the COUNTRIES and SUBDIVISIONS OF THE COUNTRIES in which they are situated. In 1 vol. large 8vo., 21s.

A NEW MAP OF EUROPE.

By A. KEITH JOHNSTON, F.R.S.E. Size, 4 feet 2 inches by 3 feet 5 inches. Cloth Case, 21s.

ATLAS OF SCOTLAND.

31 Maps of the Counties of Scotland, coloured. Bound in roan, price 10s. 6d. Each County may be had separately, in Cloth Case, 1s.

KEITH JOHNSTON'S SCHOOL ATLASES :—

GENERAL AND DESCRIPTIVE GEOGRAPHY, exhibiting the Actual and Comparative Extent of all the Countries in the World, with their present Political Divisions. A New and Enlarged Edition. With a complete Index. 26 Maps. Half-bound, 12s. 6d.

PHYSICAL GEOGRAPHY, illustrating, in a Series of Original Designs, the Elementary Facts of Geology, Hydrology, Meteorology, and Natural History. A New and Enlarged Edition. 19 Maps, including coloured Geological Maps of Europe and of the British Isles. Half-bound, 12s. 6d.

CLASSICAL GEOGRAPHY, comprising, in Twenty Plates, Maps and Plans of all the important Countries and Localities referred to by Classical Authors ; accompanied by a pronouncing Index of Places, by T. HARVEY, M.A. Oxon. A New and Revised Edition. Half-bound, 12s. 6d.

ASTRONOMY. Edited by J. R. HIND, Esq., F.R.A.S., &c. Notes and Descriptive Letterpress to each Plate, embodying all recent Discoveries in Astronomy. 18 Maps. Half-bound, 12s. 6d.

ELEMENTARY SCHOOL ATLAS OF GENERAL AND DESCRIPTIVE GEOGRAPHY for the Use of Junior Classes. A New and Cheaper Edition. 20 Maps, including a Map of Canaan and Palestine. Half-bound, 5s.

" They are as superior to all School Atlases within our knowledge, as were the larger works of the same Author in advance of those that preceded them."—Educational Times.

" Decidedly the best School Atlases we have ever seen."—English Journal of Education.

" The best, the fullest, the most accurate and recent, as well as artistically the most beautiful atlas that can be put into the schoolboy's hands."—Museum, April 1863.

A MANUAL OF MODERN GEOGRAPHY:

Mathematical, Physical, and Political. Embracing a complete Development of the River-Systems of the Globe. By the REV. ALEX. MACKAY, F.R.G.S. With Index. 7s. 6d., bound in leather.

THE BOOK OF THE FARM.

Detailing the Labours of the Farmer, Farm-Steward, Ploughman, Shepherd, Hedger, Cattle-man, Field-worker, and Dairymaid, and forming a safe Monitor for Students in Practical Agriculture. By HENRY STEPHENS, F.R.S.E. 2 vols. royal 8vo, £3, handsomely bound in cloth, with upwards of 600 , Illustrations.

"The best book I have ever met with."—*Professor Johnston.*

"We have thoroughly examined these volumes; but to give a full notice of their varied and valuable contents would occupy a larger space than we can conveniently devote to their discussion ; we therefore, in general terms, commend them to the careful study of every young man who wishes to become a good practical farmer."—*Times.*

"One of the completest works on agriculture of which our literature can boast."—*Agricultural Gazette.*

THE BOOK OF FARM IMPLEMENTS AND MACHINES.

By JAMES SLIGHT and R. SCOTT BURN. Edited by HENRY STEPHENS, F.R.S.E. Illustrated with 876 Engravings. Royal 8vo, uniform with the 'Book of the Farm,' half-bound, £2, 2s.

THE BOOK OF FARM BUILDINGS:

Their Arrangement and Construction. By HENRY STEPHENS, F.R.S.E., and R. SCOTT BURN. Royal 8vo, with 1045 Illustrations. Uniform with the 'Book of the Farm.' Half-bound, £1, 11s. 6d.

THE BOOK OF THE GARDEN.

By CHARLES M'INTOSH. In 2 large vols. royal 8vo, embellished with 1353 Engravings.

Each Volume may be had separately—viz.:

I. ARCHITECTURAL AND ORNAMENTAL.—On the Formation of Gardens— Construction, Heating, and Ventilation of Fruit and Plant Houses, Pits, Frames, and other Garden Structures, with Practical Details. Illustrated by 1073 Engravings, pp. 766. £2, 10s.

II. PRACTICAL GARDENING.—Directions for the Culture of the Kitchen Garden, the Hardy-fruit Garden, the Forcing Garden, and Flower Garden, including Fruit and Plant Houses, with Select Lists of Vegetables, Fruits, and Plants. Pp. 868, with 279 Engravings. £1, 17s. 6d.

"We feel justified in recommending Mr M'Intosh's two excellent volumes to the notice of the public." —*Gardeners' Chronicle.*

PRACTICAL SYSTEM OF FARM BOOK-KEEPING:

Being that recommended in the 'Book of the Farm' by H. STEPHENS. Royal 8vo, 2s. 6d. Also, SEVEN FOLIO ACCOUNT-BOOKS, printed and ruled in accordance with the System, the whole being specially adapted for keeping, by an easy and accurate method, an account of all the transactions of the Farm. A detailed Prospectus may be had from the Publishers. Price of the complete set of Eight Books, £1, 4s. 6d. Also, A LABOUR ACCOUNT OF THE ESTATE, 2s. 6d.

"We have no hesitation in saying that, of the many systems of keeping farm accounts which are now in vogue, there is not one which will bear comparison with this."—*Bell's Messenger.*

AINSLIE'S TREATISE ON LAND-SURVEYING.

A New and Enlarged Edition. Edited by WILLIAM GALBRAITH, M.A., F.R.A.S. 1 vol. 8vo, with a Volume of Plates in Quarto, 21s.

"The best book on surveying with which I am acquainted."—W. RUTHERFORD, LL.D., F.R.A.S., *Royal Military Academy, Woolwich.*

THE FORESTER:

A Practical Treatise on the Planting, Rearing, and Management of Forest Trees. By JAMES BROWN, Wood Manager to the Earl of Seafield. Third Edition, greatly enlarged, with numerous Engravings on Wood. Royal 8vo, 31s. 6d.

"Beyond all doubt this is the best work on the subject of Forestry extant."—*Gardeners' Journal.*

"The most useful guide to good arboriculture in the English language."—*Gardeners' Chronicle.*

HANDBOOK OF THE MECHANICAL ARTS,

Concerned in the Construction and Arrangement of Dwellings and other Buildings; Including Carpentry, Smith-work, Iron-framing, Brick-making, Columns, Cements, Well-sinking, Enclosing of Land, Road-making, &c. By R. SCOTT BURN. Crown 8vo, with 504 Engravings on Wood, 6s. 6d.

PROFESSOR JOHNSTON'S WORKS:—

EXPERIMENTAL AGRICULTURE. Being the Results of Past, and Suggestions for Future, Experiments in Scientific and Practical Agriculture. 8s.

ELEMENTS OF AGRICULTURAL CHEMISTRY AND GEOLOGY. Eighth Edition, 6s. 6d.

A CATECHISM OF AGRICULTURAL CHEMISTRY AND GEOLOGY. Fifty-seventh Edition. Edited by Dr VOELCKER. 1s.

ON THE USE OF LIME IN AGRICULTURE. 6s.

INSTRUCTIONS FOR THE ANALYSIS OF SOILS. Fourth Edition, 2s.

THE RELATIVE VALUE OF ROUND AND SAWN TIMBER,

Shown by means of Tables and Diagrams. By JAMES RAIT, Land-Steward at Castle-Forbes. Royal 8vo, 8s. half-bound.

THE YEAR-BOOK OF AGRICULTURAL FACTS.

1859 and 1860. Edited by R. SCOTT BURN. Fcap. 8vo, 5s. each. 1861 and 1862, 4s. each.

ELKINGTON'S SYSTEM OF DRAINING:

A Systematic Treatise on the Theory and Practice of Draining Land, adapted to the various Situations and Soils of England and Scotland, drawn up from the Communications of Joseph Elkington, by J. JOHNSTONE. 4to, 10s. 6d.

JOURNAL OF AGRICULTURE, AND TRANSACTIONS OF THE HIGHLAND AND AGRICULTURAL SOCIETY OF SCOTLAND.

OLD SERIES, 1828 to 1843, 21 vols.	.	.	.	£3 3 0
NEW SERIES, 1843 to 1851, 8 vols.	.	.	.	2 2 0

THE RURAL ECONOMY OF ENGLAND, SCOTLAND, AND

IRELAND. By LEONCE DE LAVERGNE. Translated from the French. With Notes by a Scottish Farmer. In 8vo, 12s.

"One of the best works on the philosophy of agriculture and of agricultural political economy that has appeared."—*Spectator.*

DAIRY MANAGEMENT AND FEEDING OF MILCH COWS:

Being the recorded Experience of MRS AGNES SCOTT, Winkston, Peebles. Second Edition. Fcap., 1s.

ITALIAN IRRIGATION:

A Report addressed to the Hon. the Court of Directors of the East India Company, on the Agricultural Canals of Piedmont and Lombardy; with a Sketch of the Irrigation System of Northern and Central India. By LIEUT.-COL. BAIRD SMITH, C.B. Second Edition. 2 vols. 8vo, with Atlas in folio, 30s.

THE ARCHITECTURE OF THE FARM:

A Series of Designs for Farm Houses, Farm Steadings, Factors' Houses, and Cottages. By JOHN STARFORTH, Architect. Sixty-two Engravings. In medium 4to, £2, 2s.

"One of the most useful and beautiful additions to Messrs Blackwood's extensive and valuable library of agricultural and rural economy."—*Morning Post.*

THE YESTER DEEP LAND-CULTURE:

Being a Detailed Account of the Method of Cultivation which has been successfully practised for several years by the Marquess of Tweeddale at Yester. By HENRY STEPHENS, Esq., F.R.S.E., Author of the ' Book of the Farm.' In small 8vo, with Engravings on Wood, 4s. 6d.

A MANUAL OF PRACTICAL DRAINING.
By HENRY STEPHENS, F.R.S.E., Author of the 'Book of the Farm.'
Third Edition, 8vo, 5s.

A CATECHISM OF PRACTICAL AGRICULTURE.
By HENRY STEPHENS, F.R S.E., Author of the 'Book of the Farm,' &c.
In crown 8vo, with Illustrations, 1s.

HANDY BOOK ON PROPERTY LAW.
By LORD ST LEONARDS. The Seventh Edition. To which is now added
a Letter on the New Laws for obtaining an Indefeasible Title. With a Portrait of the Author, engraved by HOLL. 3s. 6d.

"Less than 200 pages serve to arm us with the ordinary precautions to which we should attend in sell-
ing, buying, mortgaging, leasing, settling, and devising estates. We are informed of our relations to our
property, to our wives and children, and of our liability as trustees or executors, in a little book for the
million,—a book which the author tenders to the *profanum vulgus* as even capable of 'beguiling a few
hours in a railway carriage.'"—*Times.*

THE PLANTER'S GUIDE.
By SIR HENRY STEUART. A New Edition, with the Author's last Additions
and Corrections. 8vo, with Engravings, 21s.

STABLE ECONOMY:
A Treatise on the Management of Horses. By JOHN STEWART, V.S.
Seventh Edition, 6s. 6d.

" Will always maintain its position as a standard work upon the management of horses."—*Mark Lane
Express.*

ADVICE TO PURCHASERS OF HORSES.
By JOHN STEWART, V.S. 18mo, plates, 2s. 6d.

*A PRACTICAL TREATISE ON THE CULTIVATION OF THE
GRAPE VINE.* By WILLIAM THOMSON, Gardener to His Grace the
Duke of Buccleuch, Dalkeith Park. Third Edition. 8vo, 5s.

" When books on gardening are written thus conscientiously, they are alike honourable to their author
and valuable to the public."—*Lindley's Gardeners' Chronicle.*

" Want of space prevents us giving extracts, and we must therefore conclude by saying, that as the
author is one of the very best grape-growers of the day, this book may be stated as being the key to his
successful practice, and as such, we can with confidence recommend it as indispensable to all who wish
to excel in the cultivation of the vine."—*The Florist and Pomologist.*

*THE CHEMISTRY OF VEGETABLE AND ANIMAL PHYSI-
OLOGY.* By DR J. G. MULDER, Professor of Chemistry in the University
of Utrecht. With an Introduction and Notes by Professor JOHNSTON. 22
Plates. 8vo, 30s.

THE MOOR AND THE LOCH.
Containing Minute Instructions in all Highland Sports, with Wanderings
over Crag and Correi, Flood and Fell. By JOHN COLQUHOUN, Esq.
Third Edition. 8vo, with Illustrations, 12s. 6d.

SALMON-CASTS AND STRAY SHOTS:
Being Fly-Leaves from the Note-Book of JOHN COLQUHOUN, Esq.,
Author of 'The Moor and the Loch,' &c. Second Edition. Fcap. 8vo, 5s.

COQUET-DALE FISHING SONGS.
Now first collected by a North-Country Angler, with the Music of the Airs.
8vo, 5s.

*THE ANGLER'S COMPANION TO THE RIVERS AND LOCHS
OF SCOTLAND.* By T. T. STODDART. With Map of the Fishing Streams
and Lakes of Scotland. Second Edition. Crown 8vo, 3s. 6d.

" Indispensable in all time to come, as the very strength and grace of an angler's tackle and equipment
in Scotland, must and will be STODDART'S ANGLER'S COMPANION."—*Blackwood's Magazine.*

RELIGION IN COMMON LIFE:
A Sermon preached in Crathie Church, October 14, 1855, before Her Majesty the Queen and Prince Albert. By the Rev. JOHN CAIRD, D.D. Published by Her Majesty's Command. Bound in cloth, 8d. Cheap Edition, 3d.

SERMONS.
By the Rev. JOHN CAIRD, D.D., Professor of Divinity in the University of Glasgow, and one of Her Majesty's Chaplains for Scotland. In crown 8vo, 5s. This Edition includes the Sermon on 'Religion in Common Life,' preached in Crathie Church, Oct. 1855, before Her Majesty the Queen and the late Prince Consort.

"They are noble sermons; and we are not sure but that, with the cultivated reader, they will gain rather than lose by being read, not heard. There is a thoughtfulness and depth about them which can hardly be appreciated, unless when they are studied at leisure; and there are so many sentences so felici tously expressed that we should grudge being hurried away from them by a rapid speaker, without being allowed to enjoy them a second time."—*Fraser's Magazine.*

THE BOOK OF JOB.
By the late Rev. GEORGE CROLY, LL.D., Rector of St Stephen's, Walbrook. With a Memoir of the Author by his Son. Fcap. 8vo, 4s.

LECTURES IN DIVINITY.
By the late Rev. GEORGE HILL, D.D., Principal of St Mary's College, St Andrews. Stereotyped Edition. 8vo, 14s.

"I am not sure if I can recommend a more complete manual of Divinity."—*Dr Chalmers.*

THE MOTHER'S LEGACIE TO HER UNBORNE CHILDE.
By Mrs ELIZABETH JOCELINE. Edited by the Very Rev. Principal LEE. 32mo, 4s. 6d.

"This beautiful and touching legacie."—*Athenæum.*
"A delightful monument of the piety and high feeling of a truly noble mother."—*Morning Advertiser.*

ANALYSIS AND CRITICAL INTERPRETATION OF THE HEBREW TEXT OF THE BOOK OF GENESIS. Preceded by a Hebrew Grammar, and Dissertations on the Genuineness of the Pentateuch, and on the Structure of the Hebrew Language. By the Rev. WILLIAM PAUL, A.M. 8vo, 18s.

PRAYERS FOR SOCIAL AND FAMILY WORSHIP.
Prepared by a COMMITTEE OF THE GENERAL ASSEMBLY OF THE CHURCH OF SCOTLAND, and specially designed for the use of Soldiers, Sailors, Colonists, Sojourners in India, and other Persons, at Home or Abroad, who are deprived of the Ordinary Services of a Christian Ministry. *Published by Authority of the Committee.* Third Edition. In crown 8vo, bound in cloth, 4s.

PRAYERS FOR SOCIAL AND FAMILY WORSHIP.
Being a Cheap Edition of the above. Fcap. 8vo, 1s. 6d.

THE CHRISTIAN LIFE,
In its Origin, Progress, and Perfection. By the VERY REV. E. B. RAMSAY, LL.D., F.R.S.E., Dean of the Diocese of Edinburgh. Crown 8vo, 9s.

THEISM: THE WITNESS OF REASON AND NATURE TO AN ALL-WISE AND BENEFICENT CREATOR. By the Rev. JOHN TULLOCH, D.D., Principal and Professor of Theology, St Mary's College, St Andrews; and one of Her Majesty's Chaplains in Ordinary in Scotland. In 1 vol. 8vo, 10s. 6d.

ON THE ORIGIN AND CONNECTION OF THE GOSPELS OF MATTHEW, MARK, AND LUKE: With Synopsis of Parallel Passages, and Critical Notes. By JAMES SMITH, Esq. of Jordanhill, F.R.S., Author of the 'Voyage and Shipwreck of St Paul.' Medium 8vo, 16s.

WILLIAM BLACKWOOD AND SONS.

19

INSTITUTES OF METAPHYSIC: THE THEORY OF KNOW-ING AND BEING. By JAMES F. FERRIER, A.B. Oxon., Professor of Moral Philosophy and Political Economy, St Andrews. Second Edition. Crown 8vo, 10s. 6d.

"We have no doubt, however, that the subtlety and depth of metaphysical genius which his work betrays, its rare display of rigorous and consistent reasonings, and the inimitable precision and beauty of its style on almost every page, must secure for it a distinguished place in the history of philosophical discussion."—*Tulloch's Burnett Prize Treatise.*

LECTURES ON METAPHYSICS.
By SIR WILLIAM HAMILTON, Bart., Professor of Logic and Metaphysics in the University of Edinburgh. Edited by the Rev. H. L. MANSEL, B.D., LL.D., Waynflete Professor of Moral and Metaphysical Philosophy, Oxford; and JOHN VEITCH, M.A., Professor of Logic, Rhetoric, and Metaphysics, St Andrews. Third Edition. 2 vols. 8vo, 24s.

LECTURES ON LOGIC.
By SIR WILLIAM HAMILTON, Bart. Edited by Professors MANSEL and VEITCH. In 2 vols., 24s.

THORNDALE; OR, THE CONFLICT OF OPINIONS.
By WILLIAM SMITH, Author of 'A Discourse on Ethics,' &c. Second Edition. Crown 8vo, 10s. 6d.

"The subjects treated of, and the style—always chaste and beautiful, often attractively grand—in which they are clothed, will not fail to secure the attention of the class for whom the work is avowedly written. . . . . It deals with many of those higher forms of speculation characteristic of the cultivated minds of the age."—*North British Review.*

GRAVENHURST; OR, THOUGHTS ON GOOD AND EVIL.
By WILLIAM SMITH, Author of 'Thorndale,' &c. In crown 8vo, 7s. 6d.

"One of those rare books which, being filled with noble and beautiful thoughts, deserves an attentive and thoughtful perusal."—*Westminster Review.*

A DISCOURSE ON ETHICS OF THE SCHOOL OF PALEY.
By WILLIAM SMITH, Author of 'Thorndale.' 8vo, 4s.

ON THE INFLUENCE EXERTED BY THE MIND OVER THE BODY, in the Production and Removal of Morbid and Anomalous Conditions of the Animal Economy. By JOHN GLEN, M.A. Crown 8vo, 2s. 6d.

DESCARTES ON THE METHOD OF RIGHTLY CONDUCT-ING THE REASON, and Seeking Truth in the Sciences. Translated from the French. 12mo, 2s.

DESCARTES' MEDITATIONS, AND SELECTIONS FROM HIS PRINCIPLES OF PHILOSOPHY. Translated from the Latin. 12mo, 3s.

SPECULATIVE PHILOSOPHY:
An INTRODUCTORY LECTURE delivered at the Opening of the Class of Logic and Rhetoric in the University of Glasgow, Nov. 1, 1864. By JOHN VEITCH, M.A., Professor of Logic and Rhetoric in the University of Glasgow. 1s.

CHEAP EDITIONS OF POPULAR WORKS.

LIGHTS AND SHADOWS OF SCOTTISH LIFE.
Fcap. 8vo, 3s. cloth.

THE TRIALS OF MARGARET LYNDSAY.
By the Author of ' Lights and Shadows of Scottish Life.'
Fcap. 8vo, 3s. cloth.

THE FORESTERS.
By the Author of ' Lights and Shadows of Scottish Life.'
Fcap. 8vo, 3s. cloth.

TOM CRINGLE'S LOG.
Complete in One Volume, Fcap. 8vo, 4s. cloth.

THE CRUISE OF THE MIDGE.
By the Author of 'Tom Cringle's Log.'
In One Volume, Fcap. 8vo, 4s. cloth.

THE LIFE OF MANSIE WAUCH,
TAILOR IN DALKEITH.
Fcap. 8vo, 3s. cloth.

THE SUBALTERN.
By the Author of 'The Chelsea Pensioners.'——Fcap. 8vo, 3s. cloth.

PENINSULAR SCENES AND SKETCHES.
By the Author of ' The Student of Salamanca.'
Fcap. 8vo, 3s. cloth.

NIGHTS AT MESS, SIR FRIZZLE PUMPKIN,
AND OTHER TALES.——Fcap. 8vo, 3s. cloth.

THE YOUTH AND MANHOOD OF CYRIL THORNTON.
By the Author of ' Men and Manners in America.'
Fcap. 8vo, 4s. cloth.

VALERIUS: A ROMAN STORY.
Fcap. 8vo, 3s. cloth.

REGINALD DALTON.
By the Author of ' Valerius.'——Fcap. 8vo, 4s. cloth.

SOME PASSAGES IN THE LIFE OF ADAM BLAIR, AND HISTORY OF MATTHEW WALD.
By the Author of ' Valerius.'——Fcap. 8vo, 4s. cloth.

ANNALS OF THE PARISH, AND AYRSHIRE LEGATEES,
BY JOHN GALT.——Fcap. 8vo, 4s. cloth.

SIR ANDREW WYLIE.
By JOHN GALT.——Fcap. 8vo, 4s. cloth.

THE PROVOST, AND OTHER TALES.
By JOHN GALT.——Fcap. 8vo, 4s. cloth.

THE ENTAIL.
By JOHN GALT.——Fcap. 8vo, 4s. cloth.

LIFE IN THE FAR WEST.
By G. F. RUXTON.——A New Edition. Fcap. 8vo, 4s. cloth.

 W. BLACKWOOD & SONS, Edinburgh and London.

www.ingramcontent.com/pod-product-compliance
Lightning Source LLC
Chambersburg PA
CBHW020102030726
47498CB00006B/1907